Show You No Mercy 2

Forgiveness Won't Come Easy

K. Powell

Authentic Reads Publication

Book Cover by Black Girl Digital Labs

ISBN: 979-8-9869925-2-5 (Paperback)

ISBN: 979-8-9869925-3-2 (eBook)

AUTHENTIC READS PUBLICATION

SHOW YOU NO MERCY 2

FORGIVENESS WON'T COME EASY

K. POWELL

To those who inspire the words and breathe life into the pages, this book is dedicated with heartfelt gratitude. Your belief fuels my creativity, and your support lights my path. Here's to another chapter together.

Trigger Warning

This work contains explicit references to rape and drug abuse. Reader discretion is advised, especially for those who may find such topics distressing or triggering. Please prioritize your mental and emotional well-being. If these topics might be harmful or unsettling to you, please consider reading another story or seeking supportive resources.

Chapter 1

Clash of Worlds

"Revenge slowly consumes us from within and robs us of our peace and joy, leaving us trapped in a cycle of bitterness and resentment." - K. Powell

Sage sat on her bed, lost in thought. The events of the past few months had left her feeling drained, and she couldn't help but replay everything over and over in her mind. She stared off into space, her eyes unfocused as she tried to make sense of it all.

"Are you okay?" Avery asked, looking around Sage's messy bedroom.

She quickly regained focus and began sorting through clothes. "Yes, I'm fine. What's up?"

Around them, Sage's room was in disarray. Clothes were strewn everywhere, and opened drawers revealed a mix of accessories and papers. A few picture frames lay askew on the nightstand. Sage was clearly in the midst of tidying up, but it seemed like a daunting task.

Avery's eyes sparkled with an irrepressible joy, her young face radiant. Her heart seemed to beat right out of her chest, and every word she uttered vibrated with exhilaration. "Did you see the news? Mommy is coming home. There was an acquittal. Whatever that means." She bounced on the balls of her feet, her hands clenched in little fists of excitement, oblivious to the full weight of the word 'acquittal.'

Sage, however, went still. Her face drained of color, and she felt as if someone had yanked the ground from beneath her. Her heart thudded loudly, its rhythm disjointed. "Wait, what?" she whispered. "She really got away with it?"

Confusion clouded Avery's eyes. "Got away with what? I don't understand." She took a step closer to Sage. "Are you saying that mommy really shot Uncle Tanner?" The room seemed to close in.

"No, Avery, that is not what I'm saying. You're just too young to understand," Sage said. She looked away, her fingers subconsciously playing with the hem of her shirt.

Avery's feet shifted on the soft carpet, her sneakers made a soft rustling sound. "I am 12 years old," she retorted. "I understand a lot of things, and you're only 4 years older than me." Her eyes, usually soft and curious, held a challenging spark.

Sage's eyebrows furrowed, her face a mosaic of irritation. "What is that supposed to mean?" She placed her hand on her hip.

Matching her sister's stance, Avery squared her shoulders. "What makes you more qualified to understand something more than me?" Her voice, although still youthful, carried a weight far beyond her years.

"You're going to make a great lawyer one day because you don't ever shut up," Sage sneered.

"You shut up," Avery spat back, her cheeks flushing a deep shade of red.

Sage took a step forward, her face inches from Avery's. Their heated glares were locked, neither willing to back down. Like two magnets repelling one another, the sisters circled each other in a tight space of the room.

Avery lunged at Sage, trying to shove her. Sage, surprised, stumbled back a step but quickly retaliated and reached out to grab Avery's wrist in a tight grip. The two grappled, their struggle filling the room with sounds of shuffled feet, strained breaths, and the rustling of fabric. They knocked a forgotten book on a nearby table over, its pages scattered in a chaotic dance.

The door swung open with a force, revealing Mylan's towering figure, his broad shoulders tensed, and a stern look on his face. His eyes scanned the room, immediately taking in the scene. Sage and Avery's face flushed and their clothes disheveled, the scattered book pages, and the unmistakable tension in the air.

"Mylan," Sage breathed out, her voice barely above a whisper.

Mylan stepped between them, his large hands gently but firmly pushed them apart. "Enough," he said.

"Avery, leave the room. I need to speak with Sage," Mylan demanded.

Avery shot Sage a defiant look, hesitated for a second, then huffed out of the room and slammed the door behind her.

Mylan turned his attention back to Sage, taking a moment to gather his thoughts before speaking. "I know there have been a lot of changes in your life these past few months," he began, his tone softer now.

Sage cut him off. "I honestly don't need a pep talk right now."

Mylan raised a hand and signaled for her to wait. "Well, good, because this isn't one. I know what happened to you is hard for you to handle mentally, but-

Sage's eyes welled up, her voice shaky but fierce. "Oh, my god. Uncle Mylan, I do not want to talk about this. Can we please not talk about it?"

Mylan's face softened as he took in Sage's distraught state. The weight of their shared pain and memories lingered heavy

in the silence that followed. "Okay, my apologies," he began, his voice carried the sincerity of his words. He paused, choosing his words carefully. "How about you explain to me what that was with your sister?"

Sage's gaze dropped to the floor. "She is just annoying," she muttered. "I don't have time to deal with her. I have my own shit to worry about." Catching herself, she quickly added, "I'm sorry," her face reddening at the slip.

Mylan regarded her for a moment. "I understand where you're coming from," he began, his tone gentle. "But you also have to remember she lost a father, too. The way she's acting and the things she's doing. It's all part of her way of coping." He paused, letting his words sink in. "She's just trying to find happiness amongst all the pain. She needs you and you need her. Don't lose sight of that."

"I know but-

Mylan interrupted, "But nothing. If I could change anything from my past, I never would have sent your mother away when she was 17. I wish I would have spent more time with her and showed her a different path, but I lost time with her. You still have the chance to build a closer bond."

Sage's eyes flashed defiantly. "Your situation is different. Mom is an evil witch. She deserved to be sent away."

Mylan's stern expression broke. "Aye, watch your mouth," he smirked.

Then, with an unexpected tenderness, Mylan stepped closer, his tall frame bent slightly to meet Sage's shorter stature. He wrapped his arms around her in a gentle, yet firm, embrace. The warmth of the hug seemed to melt away the room's earlier tension, replacing it with a sense of understanding and comfort.

***

The morning sun streamed into the kitchen, cast a warm glow over the brown table set for breakfast. A medley of scents–freshly brewed coffee, toast, and scrambled eggs–filled the air. Mylan sat at the head of the table. Beside him was Sarah, her radiant pregnancy glow highlighted by the sunlight.

Across from them were Sage and Avery. Sage, with her school bag already slung over her chair, pushed around her scrambled eggs with her fork. Meanwhile, Avery was fidgeting with her food, her nervousness clear. "I don't feel so good," Avery admitted, her eyes darting towards Sage as if seeking confirmation that her feelings were valid.

"Those are just first day jitters," Sarah responded with a light-hearted giggle.

Sage's eyes rolled almost theatrically at the comment. The silver hoop in her ear glinted as she turned to her younger sister.

"What if no one likes me?" Avery muttered, her voice barely above a whisper, eyes downcast.

Sage leaned in, her voice firm, but filled with love. "Who cares if no one likes you? Screw them."

Mylan and Sarah exchanged a quick, startled glance. "It is normal to feel that way when you're entering a new school, but Sage's school is just a few blocks away," Sarah reassured.

Avery's lips pressed into a thin line. Without a word, she pushed back her chair, its legs scraped slightly against the tiled floor. She moved with a hesitant grace to the corner of the room where her bag was.

Mylan's gaze fixed on Sage. His expression shifted to one of seriousness. "I expect you to look out for your sister," he began. "Brooklyn is different from Buffalo. Not everything is going to be peaches and cream."

Sage's eyes flashed, "I don't understand why we couldn't stay upstate with Auntie Matty or Uncle Tanner. Why do we have to start all over at a new school? All of our friends are back home." Each word was like a piece of her heart laid out.

"Sage, you know-

Sage cut Sarah off sharply, her voice edged with bitterness. "No offense, but I'm not talking to you."

Mylan snapped. "Watch your mouth, little girl," his open palm slammed down on the dining table, making the plates and glasses jitter. "You need to show some respect. I could have sent both y'all asses to foster care."

Sage's shoulders squared. Her eyes, burned with a mix of anger and hurt, locked onto Mylan's. "Why didn't you?"

His response was immediate, almost instinctive. "Because I love my sister."

Mylan pulled up to the front of the school. The engine of the deep blue Dodge Charger purred softly. He reached into the glove compartment, pulled out two iPhones, and handed them to Sage and Avery. "These are for you two," he said, his voice stern but caring. "Here's some money. I've already stored our numbers in there. Call if you need anything."

Avery, her face lit up, and she quickly pocketed the phone, while Sage just nodded, her expression a tad more reserved.

Once the girls were out of the car, Mylan gave them a lingered look before driving away. Sage turned her attention to Avery. Avery's nervous energy was clear in the way she clutched her bag and adjusted her hair, but she took steady steps.

The school itself was a grand, old building, its brickwork a testament to the decades it had stood there. Ivy crawled up sections of its walls, and the large oak doors at the entrance looked like they held countless stories of past students. The hustle and bustle of the morning was clear. Students exchanged greetings, laughed, and chatted animatedly.

With Avery safely inside, Sage continued past her own school. Just a block away, she entered a worn-down park. The trees, tall but uncared for, whispered with their ragged leaves. The paths had cracks, and small groups gathered in various spots, quickly exchanged items as they hunched over a game of dice. A faint smell of stale cigarettes lingered in the air, and a distant radio played a familiar song. Despite its rough edges, the park offered Sage a temporary escape from the order of school life.

Sage was engrossed in her phone. The bright screen reflected in her eyes as she scrolled through videos. Feeling a pang of hunger, she pulled out the lunch Sarah had packed for her. Unwrapping the sandwich, she took a bite; the flavors melding together perfectly. *At least the white girl can make a good sandwich*, she thought, a hint of a smirk played on her lips.

Suddenly, a voice interrupted her thoughts. "Yo, Jordans!" The shout wasn't aggressive, but it definitely carried an assertive tone.

She lifted her gaze from her meal. Sage locked eyes with a girl pointing at her sneakers. The girl had a playful grin, her stance confident. "What's up?" Sage replied, her voice measured and cool.

"Me and my homegirls were just talking about your outfit," the girl remarked, as she nodded towards a group of girls that stood a little distance away. All of them observed the exchange with keen interest.

Sage inclined her head slightly, her lips curved in a polite smile. "Thank you," she replied gracefully.

"I'm really feeling them sneakers, though. Where you cop those from?" the girl continued, her eyes lingered on Sage's shoes.

Sage crossed one ankle over the other, as she displayed her Jordans with casual pride. "Got them from a store called Fresh Kicks," she shared, her posture relaxed.

The girl's expression shifted, a glint of something more calculated in her eyes. "How about you come up off those? I'm sure you'll get another pair. You look like your family got some money."

Sage's eyebrows knitted together, her poised demeanor replaced with genuine confusion. "I don't understand what you mean. Come up off what?"

The girl's impatience bubbled over, her voice dripped with disdain. "Are you dumb? Give me your damn sneakers or we're taking them from you."

Sage's response was immediate. She pushed herself to her feet, her full height now on display, as she locked eyes with the girl. "I'm not dumb, but you obviously are if you think I'm giving you my sneakers. Maybe if you got a job, you wouldn't be out here trying to rob people."

The tension grew palpable as the girl's crew circled, as they formed a tight ring around Sage. The murmurs among them hinted at anticipation, their body language collectively defensive and hostile.

"Who you think you're talking to?" The girl's voice held an edge sharper than before.

"The bum trying to rob me," Sage shot back.

With a swift movement, fueled by anger, the girl reached out, her fingers curled tightly into the fabric of Sage's sweater, as she yanked her closer. The two of them were now nose-to-nose.

"Aye, chill out!" A commanding voice rang out.

From the fringes of the park, a figure approached. Kamari, with her confident stride, made her way through the park's paths. Her presence alone drew attention. As she neared the tense circle, she didn't hesitate to walk right into its center and broke the barrier the girls had created around Sage.

The aura around Kamari was visible; there was a respect, perhaps even a hint of fear, that her presence commanded. "Do we have a problem?" Kamari's voice was steady.

A few inaudible mutters were the only replies, but within moments, the group scattered, the instigator who threw one last glare at Sage before she departed.

As the tension diffused, Kamari turned to Sage. Sage took a moment to steady herself after the confrontation and gathered her belongings. "Thanks," she murmured.

"I've never seen you before. What are you doing around here by yourself?" Kamari questioned.

"I go to school up the block," Sage replied, as she gestured vaguely in the direction she had come from.

Kamari's gaze traveled over Sage as she took in her attire, her posture, every nuance that might tell her more about this newcomer. "I'm Kamari," she introduced herself with a certain pride in her tone, "You ain't from Brooklyn."

Sage's eyebrows raised slightly at the declaration. Her lips curved in a half-smile. "Was that a statement or a question?" she retorted playfully.

A genuine chuckle escaped Kamari's lips. "And you've got a smart-ass mouth. So, where you from, smart mouth?"

As she took in a breath, Sage responded, "I'm Sage. Originally from Buffalo."

Sage glanced at her watch. "I've got to head out and pick up my sister," she said, as she turned toward the school. To her surprise, Kamari fell into step beside her. The park was now behind them. "I don't need a bodyguard. I can handle myself," Sage declared.

Kamari shot her a side glance. A smirk played at the corner of her mouth. "Obviously, you do because you almost got your ass beat by those girls. Trust me, you don't want to make enemies out of them."

Sage stopped in her tracks and forced Kamari to halt as well. The two faced each other on the bustling sidewalk. "So, what about you?" Sage inquired, her eyes searching Kamari's.

Kamari raised an eyebrow, intrigued by the sudden shift. "What about me?"

"How come they don't bother you?" Sage's said.

Kamari's face grew serious, and her tone dropped. "Because I am not to be played with!"

The gravity in Kamari's tone momentarily caught Sage off guard. Sage couldn't help but laugh when Kamari tried to intimidate her, despite the gravity in Kamari's tone. "What are you supposed to be, some kind of gangster?"

Kamari smirked, her eyes narrowed slightly. "I'm the person you don't want as an enemy."

Kamari made a threat, but they kept walking to the middle school through busy streets. Trying to navigate the uneasy silence between them, Kamari ventured, "Where you stay at?"

Sage blinked, thrown by the unfamiliar phrasing. "Where I stay at? I don't understand what you mean."

Kamari rolled her eyes, a playful grin formed on her face. "Damn, girl! Where you from? If you're gonna live in Brooklyn, at least learn the slang. I'm asking where you live."

Sage squared her shoulders, "None of your business. I don't know you."

A slow and appreciative smile crept across Kamari's face. "I like you."

The declaration took Sage slightly off-guard, responded reflexively, "Sorry, I'm not a lesbian."

Kamari laughed as she held up her hands defensively. "First, I ain't either. I meant I could use a girl like you on my team."

Before Sage could question Kamari's intentions, a familiar face emerged from the sea of students that poured out of the school. Avery, as her backpack bounced behind her, made her way towards Sage. Sage said quickly, "I have to go." She reached out, griped Avery's hand firmly. Without waiting for a response, the two hurried away, and left Kamari as she watched after them.

* * *

As Sage and Avery stepped through the front door, the cozy warmth of their new home. Mylan, with his imposed figure, stood near the entrance. His eyes scanned both girls. "Avery, head to your room," he instructed. Sage found herself squared off against not just Mylan but also Sarah, who stood slightly behind him with a concerned expression painted on her face. "What's up?" Sage ventured.

Mylan's pierced gaze met hers. "I don't know, you tell me. How was the first day?"

Sage shifted her weight from one foot to the other. Her gaze dropped to the floor. "It was alright. I just want to lie down. I'm tired," she murmured, her fingers fidgeted at her sides.

Mylan's keen observation skills noticed the slight changes in her demeanor. "Your school called."

Sarah stepped forward and placed a calm hand on Mylan's shoulder, her voice soft but firm. "Let's just sit down and talk about this."

But Mylan wasn't having it. "Ain't shit to talk about. Where were you?"

Sage's eyes narrowed. "What I do is none of your business. You are not my father. I just met you," she snapped.

Mylan's anger simmered. Sarah tried to defuse the tension. "You both need to calm down. Arguing will not solve the problem," she implored.

Sage's eyes locked onto Mylan's, each step she took towards him filled with defiance. "I hate you; I hate my mother; I hate this place and I hate that school. You can't make me go back," she spat out. Each word dripped with venom.

Sarah stepped between the two, her fingers gently brushed Sage's shoulder. "Just sit down, let's talk," she cooed.

But Sage, on the edge, pushed Sarah away, her movement sudden and forceful. The unexpected aggression caught everyone off guard, and in a reflexive response, Mylan's hand connected with Sage's cheek. The sound echoed in the tight confines of the room.

Sage's hand flying to her reddened cheek, her eyes filled with tears. Without another word, she bolted. Her footsteps echoed down the hallway until the soft thud of her bedroom door signaled her retreat.

A heavy silence settled in the room. Sarah turned her gaze to Mylan. Mylan's posture slumped, the weight of his action pressed down on him. "I have to speak to her. I didn't mean to," he murmured.

Sarah approached him slowly, her fingers tenderly traced circles on his shoulder, a gesture meant to comfort. "If you speak to her now, it will probably do more damage than good. Let's just sleep on it," she advised.

Chapter 2

Fragile

Sage walked into the main office, her eyes scanned the unfamiliar surroundings. She was handed a student schedule and told to wait. A moment later, a bubbly girl with a bright smile approached her.

"Hi! I'm Tegan," the girl announced as she extended a hand. "I'll be showing you around."

"You have a pretty good locker," Tegan began as they walked the corridors, "Close to the bathroom and close to the exit. You never want a locker near the gym, though. The smell after P.E.? Gross."

"Cool," Sage replied, her tone indifferent.

She sensed Sage's reluctance to chat, but still tried to make a connection. "I know this might not be any of my business, but-"

"If it's none of your business, then why are you about to ask?" Sage interrupted, her patience running thin.

Tegan winced, taken aback. "My apologies. I was just trying to help," she said as she quickly changed the topic. "That door there? That's the office of our school psychiatrist, Ms. Collen. If you ever need someone to talk to, she's outstanding."

Sage's attention was then caught by a tall guy striding confidently down the hallway. Tegan, noting her interest, smirked. "That's Cylus Wesley. Basketball prodigy. He's got NBA dreams."

"Is there a girls' basketball team?" Sage questioned.

"Sure is! They have tryouts this week. Honestly, they've been pretty bad lately. They could use some fresh talent." Tegan informed her.

After showing Sage her class, the two parted ways. The school day ended quickly for Sage, who was still adjusting to her new environment.

As she left the building, a familiar voice called out. "Yo, Buffalo!" Kamari greeted, grinning.

Sage rolled her eyes, her patience already tested today. "What do you want?"

Kamari, unfazed, continued, "Come on, Buffalo. How was school?"

"I need to get my sister," Sage replied curtly.

Kamari laughed, "Relax. You've got time. Come chill at the park."

Sage, feeling cornered, frowned. "How do you even know when my sister gets out?"

"I was with you, remember? Just come." Kamari urged.

Reluctantly, Sage followed. Kamari introduced her to a group lounging in the park. Sage stiffened, feeling out of place amongst the older crowd.

Kamari noticed and passed her a blunt. "Loosen up," she coaxed. Sage declined. Her gaze drifted to her phone to check the time.

"They're good people. Trust," Kamari assured.

Sage shifted uncomfortably. "Which school did you go to?"

Kamari laughed. "I'm 20 and went to Eddison Mathis. And nah, I didn't do the whole college thing. It wasn't for me. Barely made it through Eddison, to be honest."

Sage frowned, "You're 20? Why are you hanging around with me? I'm only 16."

Kamari's demeanor shifted, her patience thinning. "I saved your ass the other day, remember? But if you can't appreciate that, you can just leave."

Sage's eyes widened. "Are you serious?"

Kamari's voice dropped, menace creeping in. "Just get out of here. And stay out of this park."

Embarrassed and feeling vulnerable, Sage quickly retreated. Her thoughts whirled.

* * *

The soft glow of the evening light filtered through the curtains, cast a muted golden hue on the room's lavender walls. Sage's room was modest in design, with a few scattered posters of basketball players, and a bookshelf filled with trophies and medals from the games she played in Buffalo.

Sarah tapped gently on the door before she slowly pushed it open, revealing herself holding a small bible close to her chest. Its leather-bound cover seemed to have been worn out from years of usage, giving it an aura of wisdom and serenity.

"How was school today?" Sarah ventured, as she took a tentative step inside.

"It was cool," Sage replied, as she avoided Sarah's eyes. There was a pang of guilt evident in her voice as she added, "I'm thinking about trying out for the basketball team."

Sarah's face lit up. "That's amazing." She paused.

The room fell into an awkward silence, only to be broken by both of them saying, "Sorry," almost in unison.

Sarah's eyebrows raised in surprise. "Why are you saying sorry?"

Sage looked down and twirled her fingers. "I shouldn't have pushed you the other day. It was wrong." The room, filled with soft hues and memories of the past, seemed to watch as the two tried to mend their relationship.

The scent of lavender and vanilla candles wafted through the air, which made the air calm despite the tense talk happening. "I understand that this is a hard transition for you and Avery. Especially you after all that you have endured. How do you feel about your mother's acquittal?"

Sage looked at an old family photograph on her nightstand, where happier times were captured. "Honestly, I wish she went to jail. I hate her."

Sarah tilted her head, trying to read deeper into Sage's eyes, which seemed to hold a deafened sea of emotions. "What happened between you two?"

Shadows danced across Sage's face as the flickering candlelight played on her face. She hesitated, her lips quivered, "I just feel like if she hadn't made those choices when she was young, none of this would have happened."

Sarah leaned forward, her fingers brushed a tattered diary on her desk, perhaps once a confidant for young Sage. "Like you said, she was young. We all make mistakes when we're young. Even you. As we get older, we have to learn to forgive ourselves and others."

Sage's fingers clenched into tight fists, and her posture became rigid. "I would never hurt someone that I love, so I can't forgive that."

In Sarah's hand, she held a well-worn Bible, its pages slightly yellowed from time and use. She handed it to Sage, as she pointed to a specific passage, "Roman 12:19."

Sage's eyes skimmed over the words, the gravity of the verse sinking in.

Sarah's voice, gentle yet firm, broke the silence. "I want you to remember that forgiveness isn't for the other person, but for you. You can't hold on to that pain forever. It'll change you, mold you into someone you don't recognize."

Before Sage could process Sarah's words or respond, the door opened abruptly. Mylan stepped in, his tall silhouette filling the doorway. Sarah sensed the need for a private conversation, gave Sage a smile and exited. For a moment, Mylan and Sage just stared at each other. The colorful posters on the walls and the rhythmic tick of the wall clock seemed almost too loud in the silence between them.

Breaking the silence, Mylan murmured, "Mah fault for putting my hands on you. I'm still getting used to this whole being a parent thing. I forgot I should be your uncle first. I don't want you ever feeling like you can't talk to me. I'm here, whatever, whenever."

Sage's eyes, wet with unshed tears, locked onto his. Her voice quivered as she replied, "I'm sorry for being a brat. I promise I won't skip school again." The walls of resentment and misunderstanding seemed to crumble a little.

Chapter 3

Torn

Sage approached the school's gymnasium and scanned for the signup sheet for the girls' basketball team. They crowded the board with names scribbled in various handwriting. As Sage took a deep breath, she scribbled down her own name, feeling a rush of excitement mixed with nervousness.

At lunch, the cafeteria buzzed with chatter and the clatter of trays and cutlery. Sage sat with Tegan at a corner table. Tegan made a face, pushing her tray away with disgust. "The lunch is absolutely atrocious," she said. "Usually, I bring my own lunch, but I had to pick between being late or missing my geometry test. I chose the scholar route."

Sage chuckled and shook her head at Tegan's theatrical flair. Their laughter broke the initial awkwardness of their budding friendship.

Tegan leaned in and hesitated before she asked, "Since we're getting to know each other... Can I ask you something?"

Sage raised an eyebrow and signaled for Tegan to continue.

Tegan took a deep breath. "Don't get upset, but I usually do some research on all the new students... Did your mom really shoot her partner?"

Sage froze, her face drained of color. She darted her eyes around the lunchroom and hoped no one else had overheard Tegan's question. The cheerful atmosphere she had felt just moments ago quickly evaporated, replaced by an all too familiar weight in her chest.

Tegan nonchalantly bit into the banana she'd just retrieved from her bag. "Oh, don't worry," she assured, and waved off the tension with her other hand. "Nobody gives a damn about any cops getting shot." She paused as she noticed the discomfort in Sage's eyes. "I understand if you don't want to talk about it."

Sage hesitated before she replied, "It's not just that. I don't want to be known as the daughter of a former cop. I just want to be... Sage."

Tegan nodded sympathetically. "I get that. And I'm sorry for prying. Whenever you're ready to share, I'm here."

Sage's attention diverted to the cafeteria entrance.. Cylus, the much-talked-about basketball captain, strutted in. Sage tried to appear disinterested, but Tegan caught the subtle glint in her eyes. "Somebody's got a crush," Tegan teased, her grin stretched from ear to ear.

Sage ignored the remark and focused on her lunch as she took a bite of her sandwich.

Tegan nudged Sage gently. "Word is, he's throwing a massive party this weekend. His folks have this swanky place out on Long Island."

Sage's fork paused midway to her mouth. "Long Island? I don't even know where that is," she admitted. "And I doubt my uncle would let me go to some random party."

Tegan rolled her eyes playfully. "Just ask him. You might be surprised. Besides, it's THE party. Everyone's going."

Despite her reluctance, Sage couldn't hide the curiosity in her eyes. The thought of attending such an event stirred with apprehension.

Inside the gym, the repetitive thud of a basketball echoed through the space, as Sage, who was determined and focused, shot hoops alone during her free period. Each bounce of the ball drowned out the noise from her chaotic life.

From the gym's entrance, a figure walked in and cast a tall shadow that reached Sage before he did. It was Cylus, who quietly took a seat on the bleachers, and observed her moves without uttering a word.

After a few moments, he finally broke his silence. "Your stance is a little off. Spread your feet apart a bit more," he advised, his tone more curious than critical.

Sage, slightly caught off guard, pivoted to face him. Her eyes narrowed. "I don't need any advice," she said defiantly. "I've been hooping for years."

Cylus merely raised an eyebrow. A playful smirk played on his lips. "Your shot would be a lot easier."

With that challenge in the air, Sage aimed and shot. The ball circled the rim and then rolled off, not making it through.

"Told you," Cylus chuckled, his tone light.

The miss appeared to have a deeper impact on Sage than just a failed attempt at a basket. Her shoulders slumped, and she threw the ball down in frustration and turned to leave the court.

Cylus reached out and lightly grabbed her arm. Sage did not expect the contact, flinched away sharply. Cylus immediately raised his hands in a defensive gesture. "Sorry, I didn't mean to."

Sage stood frozen for a moment, her breath slightly erratic.

"Are you okay?" Cylus asked, his voice filled with genuine concern.

Sage stared at him and her voice trembled slightly as she uttered, "Don't ever touch me again."

Cylus swallowed hard, his earlier playfulness replaced by evident regret. "My bad. I just wanted to say, keep shooting until you get it right. One missed shot shouldn't discourage you."

Her eyes glistened. She mumbled, "Maybe basketball isn't for me like I thought it was."

With a deep breath, Cylus picked up the ball and dribbled a few times. "You give up that easily, huh?"

She shot him a defiant glare. "You don't know me, so watch your mouth."

In response, Cylus swiftly aimed and shot a perfect 3-pointer. He then retrieved the ball and tossed it to Sage. "Try again and spread your feet apart like I suggested."

Sage adjusted her stance, took aim, and released. The ball sailed through the air and swished through the net. The corners of her lips slowly turned upwards into a triumphant smile.

Cylus's hand shot up, animated by the thrill of her success, prepared to give her a high five. But just as quickly, he checked himself as he remembered her earlier discomfort. His hand hung uncertain midair.

Sage sensed his caution. She softened her stance. She met his gesture, slapped her hand against his. "I guess you were right," she admitted. "I have to freshen up before my next class. Thanks for the advice."

As she turned to leave, Cylus's gaze lingered on her. The weight of their brief yet impactful interaction was evident in his eyes. He watched her until she disappeared from the gym.

Sage sat silent across from Ms. Collen, the school psychiatrist. Soft lighting created a serene atmosphere, but the tension was palpable. Bookshelves lined with psychology texts and comforted by plants framed the room, but Sage's focus was elsewhere.

"I know it was your uncle's idea for you to speak to me about what is bothering you. However it has been our third session and you have not said a word." Ms. Collen's voice was kind, but her observation was sharp.

Sage shifted uncomfortably. Her eyes darted everywhere except in Ms. Collen's direction.

In a deft move, Ms. Collen reached into her drawer, and pulled out a familiar deck of Uno cards. "Would you like to play?"

A ghost of a smile tugged at the corners of Sage's lips. She sat up straighter and nodded. "Yeah."

Cards shuffled, and soon the game began. With each card laid, Ms. Collen attempted to build a bridge. "So, tell me what it was like living in Buffalo?"

A distant yet fond look crossed Sage's face. "We had a huge backyard. Avery and I used to set up a tent and pretend that we were in the woods." Sage chuckled at the memory.

Ms. Collen's face brightened and mirrored Sage's amusement. "Sounds like so much fun," she said as she put down a yellow four card.

"It was," Sage reminisced, her voice took a warmer tone. "Every year we had a different theme for Christmas. My favorite was Grinchmas. We all would dress up as the Grinch and reenact scenes from the movie. It was perfect." Sage confidently put down her card, as she declared, "Uno."

Ms. Collen nodded, as she absorbed Sage's words while she contemplated her next move. "When was it not perfect?"

Sage's face tightened, and her eyes glazed over momentarily. She swiftly put down her last card. "Uno out."

As the distant bell signaled the end of their session, Sage rose from her chair, her movements swift. She made her way to the door, hand rested on the door handle, but paused. With a deep inhale, she turned her gaze back to Ms. Collen. Her eyes bore a weight far beyond her years. "When my father was murdered."

* * *

As the door to the condo creaked open, Sage and Avery stepped in. Their footsteps barely made a sound on the polished tile floor. The dim ambient light from the setting sun bathed the living area, as it highlighted the silhouette of a familiar figure seated at the dining table. It was Nora.

Avery's eyes lit up instantly. "Mommy!" She exclaimed, her voice filled with joy, rushed forward, her small feet pitter-pattered against the floor.

Sage, however, stiffened. Her eyes, distant, met Nora's briefly before she turned away. Her eyes were dull and guarded, shadows formed underneath them. Sage's mouth turned into a firm, almost grim line as she tightly pressed her lips together. She made her way towards her room, every step heavy with emotion.

As Sage entered her room, Sarah's voice, gentle yet firm, broke the obvious tension. "Before you go in there, please have an open mind," she said to Nora.

Nora, her posture straight and her face set, shot back defiantly, "I don't need you or anybody else telling me how to raise my daughters."

Mylan stepped forward and the muscles in his arm tensed. "Well, we have been raising your daughters for the past few months, so show my wife some respect."

Nora gently tapped on Sage's door, but without waiting for any response, she entered as she displayed an air of authority. The instant intrusion on Sage's personal space immediately put the teenager on the defensive.

"Always entering rooms you're not wanted in," Sage spat, her eyes narrowed in disdain.

Nora's eyes looked pained, yet resolute. She moved to sit on the edge of Sage's bed; the mattresses dipped slightly under her weight. The room was filled with a tension you could almost touch. "We need to have a talk."

Sage's face tightened, "Yea let's talk. Let's talk about you killing my father."

The air grew colder, more electric. "Lower your damn tone," Nora snapped, suddenly on her feet, her posture one of dominance.

But Sage wasn't to be cowed. She shot up and mirrored her mother's stance. "I will talk as loud as I want to. Avery may think you're the best mom in the world, but you and I both know you ain't shit."

Nora's emotions briefly spiraled out of control. For a moment, her hand formed a tight fist, her knuckles white, only to relax a moment later, as she reminded herself of who she was dealing with. "Sage, I have changed. I will be a better mother to you and Avery."

Sage was in no mood for empathy. "You can't even be honest with me and tell me why you did it."

Nora exhaled deeply, her shoulders slumped. "I did it because I was selfish and only thinking about myself. I didn't want Henry exposing me for who I truly was."

"Who are you?" Sage questioned, voice low and dangerous.

Nora hesitated, her posture tense, the muscles in her neck visible. She looked away from her daughter, her gaze found a spot on the floor. "I was a criminal," she admitted, her voice tinged with shame. "I joined the police force to keep a closer eye on the investigations and make sure that my tracks were well hidden," Nora confessed, with a hint of shame in her voice. "All that changed when I shot that guy in the store."

Sage's laugh was sharp and cutting, a mocking sound that dripped with bitterness. Her eyes sparkled. "A dirty cop." her tone dripped with sarcasm. "You're pathetic."

The room was thick with tension, each word added weight to the air. Sage's eyes shimmered with the storm of emotions within her. She took a step back from Nora and created a physical barrier. Her posture was rigid, arms crossed over her chest.

"I will let you have that because I know you're upset," Nora said, her voice trembled but stern. "But you got one more time to disrespect me. Remember, I am still your mother."

"You stopped being my mother when you killed my father," Sage spat back, her chin raised defiantly, eyes glistened with unshed tears. "You might as well have shot him yourself."

The heavy silence was evident. Nora's hands, outstretched in an attempt at a connection, fell to her sides. Her shoulders sagged, and there was a weariness in her eyes. "I can fix this. I can make us better," she whispered.

Tears streamed down Sage's face as she screamed, "I was raped! You can't fix that. You can't make it better. This isn't irreversible."

Nora, her face etched with pain, reached out instinctively as she tried to close the space between them. But as she neared, Sage violently recoiled. The two stood apart, a pit of pain and memories separated them.

"Baby, we are a family. We have to stick together," Nora implored.

Sage's back stiffened. Without turning around, she replied coldly, "Did you think about our family when you were committing your crimes?" Her voice dripped with disgust, and she slowly turned her head to give Nora an icy glance over her shoulder. Then, turned her back once more to Nora, she whispered, "Get out of my room."

Nora stood frozen, her heart and hope shattered in that moment. The gap between them had widened further, and it seemed impossible to bridge. With a defeated sigh, she slowly turned and made her way out.

On Mylan's balcony, the muted glow from the streetlights below cast a soft illumination, made the shadows dance and weave between the two. The chilly night air carried a slight humidity, and the distant sound of city life played a faint backdrop to their intense conversation.

"How did the conversation go with Sage?" Mylan inquired.

Nora sighed deeply, her shoulders slumped under the weight of her guilt. "She's upset and has every right to be. I messed up."

Mylan hesitated for a moment, as he chose his words carefully. "Did you even have time to ask her why she didn't testify against Warren?"

Nora's eyes evaded his gaze. Her fingers nervously traced the railing of the balcony. "No, but I think I know why."

Mylan's brows furrowed. "That guy is walking around scot-free after he killed Henry. He let his soldiers take the fall for everything. What reason would she have not to testify against him?"

A pained expression crossed Nora's face. "First, you know what Bunky did to her, so of course she would testify against him. But I know her. She wasn't going to send her biological father to jail, no matter how much she hates him."

Mylan blew out a heavy breath. He ran a hand through his hair, exasperation clear in his posture. "I'm not a teenage girl, so I don't know what is possibly going through her mind. For now, just let it be. Give her some time. I'm sure she will come around." Mylan lifted his glass, the amber liquid inside shimmering under the balcony light. "Let's toast to you being home," he said.

She clinked her glass against his. "I still can't believe Tanner lied on the stand to protect me."

Mylan smirked as he took a sip of his drink. "He lost his job, but he's white, so he got to keep his pension."

Nora snorted as she tried to contain her laughter. "It's funny because it's true."

A glance between them replaced the past tension with joy from shared humor.

Chapter 4

Nightfall

The glory of Cylus's home was evident as soon as Sage and Tegan stepped inside. The strobe lights flickered as it painted the large living room in changing hues, while the thump bass vibrated the floor beneath their feet. "Wow, I didn't think Cylus was living like this," Sage exclaimed, her voice almost drowned out by the deafening music.

Tegan leaned in, and grinned cheekily, "I told you it was a big ass house!"

The party was lit. Groups of people chatted, drinks in hand. In one corner, they had set up a makeshift bar, as it served an array of colorful cocktails. The most captivating sight was in the center: a sea of dancing bodies moved rhythmically to the beat.

Tegan caught up in the infectious energy, grabbed Sage's hand and pulled her onto the dance floor. They laughed as they let the music guide their movements. The atmosphere was electric, and for that moment, all of Sage's troubles felt miles away.

They moved away from the pounding music. Tegan led Sage to the kitchen. The kitchen was filled with more of their classmates; some searched the fridge for mixers, while others stood around as they chatted. The table was laden with an assortment of bottles–vodka, rum, whiskey, and more.

Tegan poured herself a drink, then filled another cup for Sage. Sage took a sip and immediately grimaced, her face twisted in disgust. "Oh, my god. That was terrible." She spit the vile liquid back into her red cup.

Tegan's eyebrows shot up in surprise. Amusement danced in her eyes. "Wait, you've never had liquor before?"

Sage shook her head. "No, I don't drink." Her attention then drifted to a corner of the kitchen, where a small group was huddled together. Her eyes widened in shock. "What are they doing?"

Tegan followed her gaze and smirked. "The crackheads of the school." She noticed the curiosity and alarm on Sage's face. She leaned in and asked, "Wait, do you want to try it?"

A haunted memory flashed in Sage's mind, cast a shadow over her features. "I already have," she replied, her voice barely more than a whisper, the memory of when Warren forced her to sniff cocaine off the floor still fresh.

Tegan's playful demeanor dropped instantly. She stared at Sage. "You've never drank liquor before, but you did cocaine? That's... interesting." The light atmosphere had shifted, replaced by an awkward tension.

Cylus's familiar voice interrupted Tegan and Sage's conversation. "What's up, Ms. I've been playing ball my whole life, so I can't take constructive criticism." He greeted Sage with a smirk.

Tegan's eyebrows knit together in confusion, and Sage merely rolled her eyes. Seeing Tegan's puzzled look, Cylus explained, "Just a brief interaction in the gym earlier. No biggie."

With a little laugh, Tegan said, "Interesting." She spotted a group of her friends that waved her over. "I'll leave you two to catch up," she said, as she winked at Sage before she headed off.

"Thanks for coming to my party. What do you think of my place?" Cylus beamed, stretching his arms out to show off the surrounding extravagance.

"It's alright. I've seen bigger," Sage teased.

Cylus gasped and clutched his chest dramatically. Tegan overheard the exchange and nudged Sage playfully. She caught the hint and added with a chuckle, "I mean, it's nice. Do your parents even know you're throwing a party here?"

Cylus leaned in closer, and lowered his voice, "I keep my parents on a need-to-know basis, and trust me, they don't need to know about this."

Before their conversation could progress further, a lanky boy approached, and extended a small bag of white powder towards Cylus. "Want some?" he offered. Cylus declined with a wave of his hand, but the boy persisted, then turned to Sage. "How about you?"

She hesitated, her face betraying a feeling of discomfort. The boy insisted and pressed the bag into her hand. Instead of throwing it away, Sage discreetly slipped it into her pocket.

Cylus noticed the discomfort in Sage's face and extended his hand. "How about we go somewhere quieter?" he suggested.

Sage glanced over her shoulder and caught Tegan's eye. She signaled with a slight nod, indicating her intention to follow Cylus. Sage grasped his hand. She let him lead her through the energetic mob of their classmates.

The pair approached the top of a dimly lit staircase, which led to the basement. Cylus seemed to sense her hesitation. "You good? It's just the game room," he reassured.

She took a moment before she responded, "Can we just go to your room instead?"

He then escorted her upstairs to his personal space. Cylus's room was an organized chaos: a contrast of clean lines and scattered junk. The walls boasted an assortment of posters, from basketball legends to classic movies. An impressive collection of sneakers lined one side, and a prominent shelf displayed a multitude of trophies. "Where were you before Brooklyn?" Cylus inquired, breaking the silence.

"Buffalo," Sage replied wistfully. "I'd give anything to go back."

"Why don't you?"

Her face hardened momentarily. "Family issues."

He nodded empathetically. "I get that. Family issues are something I'm well acquainted with."

As she took a seat on a comfortable gaming chair, she commented, "Seems like you're living every teenager's dream."

A bittersweet smile played on Cylus's lips. "I'd trade all of this for a two-bedroom apartment in Brooklyn, if it meant seeing my parents more often."

"You wish for more time with your folks, while I couldn't care less if mine were in my life," Sage responded with a dry laugh.

A frown crossed Cylus face. "What happened?"

Her gaze wandered to the gleaming trophies. "You've got quite the collection."

Shifting topics, Cylus eagerly shared, "My dad always says I've been playing basketball since I could walk. I'm part of this street basketball team in Brooklyn. You should come watch."

As he approached her, the distance between them evaporated, she abruptly turned. The proximity, the unexpected closeness, charged the air with palpable tension.

Sage backpedaled slightly. "This street basketball team—do you play for money?"

He shrugged. "I don't, but some teammates do. They need it more than me."

Sage's wheels visibly turned, intrigued by the idea of leveraging basketball for cash. Just as Cylus began to warn her about the dangers of street basketball, a frantic Tegan burst into the room.

"5-0 just pulled up! Sage, we have to bounce!"

Cylus's eyes widened in alarm. "Use the back door!" he commanded.

Without wasting another second, Sage and Tegan bolted from the room, dashed downstairs, and fled through the rear exit. As adrenaline pumped through their veins, they scaled the backyard fence and made a hasty escape.

Sage and Tegan stumbled out of the Long Island train. As they giggled uncontrollably, their laughter echoed in the late-night station's near emptiness. "I can't believe we jumped a fence. That was so exhilarating!" Sage exclaimed, her eyes gleamed with mischief.

"If you think that's exciting, wait until you jump a turnstile and have to run from the police," Tegan said with a smirk as she playfully nudged her friend.

The two shared a brief, tight embrace, their laughter still lingered in the air. "Text me when you get home, okay?" Tegan whispered in Sage's ear.

Sage nodded as she pulled out her phone. Its screen illuminated the dark platform. "12:00 am," it read. She sighed, knowing she was still a fifteen-minute walk from home. When she looked up again, Tegan had already vanished into the distance.

Suddenly, a mocking voice cut through the night, "Yo, Jordans."

A shiver ran down Sage's spine. She turned to face the voice but saw no one. Instead of investigating, she quickened her pace, and hope to lose whoever was following her.

Then the pound of footsteps grew louder. "Not again," she thought, panic building.

She found herself encircled before she could react. The familiar faces from a previous encounter emerged from the shadows, their intentions clear in their menacing grins. At the forefront was the girl she remembered all too well. The one she'd labeled a 'bum.'

"Remember me? The bum," the girl spat out sarcastically, her eyes narrowed in anger.

"I just want to go home," Sage replied, her voice wavered.

The girl mockingly mimicked her, then sneered, "Okay then, go." But as Sage took a step, the girl added, "Wait, first give me those Jordans."

"No," Sage retorted, her voice trembled.

In an instant, two girls from the group lunged at her and pinned her against the cold, graffiti-covered station wall. Sage's heart raced, her mind frantic as she tried to wriggle free, but their grip was unyielding.

"You should've just handed them over," the main girl taunted, her voice dripped with malice.

They knocked the wind out of Sage as a brutal punch landed in her stomach. She struggled to breathe and gasped for air, but the blows kept coming. They threw her to the ground. Her vision blurred as kicks and punches rained down on her. As they ripped her shoes off, the world faded, and soon, Sage lost consciousness, the cruel laughter of her attackers the last thing she heard.

Chapter 5

Whispers

The bleak light from the hospital room's fluorescent bulbs cast a pale glow over Sage as she lay motionless in her bed. Each bruise on her face, a dark blotch of purple and blue, told a silent tale of the violence she had faced. The gentle beeping of the heart monitor was the only sound, proof that she was still with us.

Nearby, the tension between Nora and Mylan was evident. Their whispered but fierce argument contrasted with the quiet of the room.

"Why the hell would you allow her to go to a party on Long Island?" Nora's voice cracked with anger. "Sage doesn't even know the ins and outs of Brooklyn, let alone Long Island. I entrusted my children to you, and look where we are!"

Mylan's face contorted with frustration. "Are you fucking kidding me right now?" he shot back, and gestured towards Sage. "Do you think with a pregnant wife at home, I have the time or patience to deal with the bride of chucky? She said the party was in Brooklyn. Was I supposed to chain her to a bedpost?"

"You should've consulted me! My children, my rules!" Nora retorted, her eyes shined with unshed tears.

Mylan took a deep breath to stay calm. "Your children are under my roof, Nora. Maybe it's time we revisited this arrangement."

Nora looked hurt. "You know Sage can't be around me right now. She's angry."

Mylan's eyes narrowed suspiciously. "What really happened that night of the exchange with Warren? Why was she so mad at you? What did you do, Nora?"

She shook her head and looked away. "I've told you. She blames me for everything that went down that night."

A grim realization dawned on Mylan. His voice quivered. "You did something that night, didn't you?"

Nora's eyes darted nervously and avoided his gaze. "What are you talking about? Did what?" Her evasive response only deepened the chasm of distrust between them."

The heated emotions that swirled between Mylan and Nora starkly contrasted the cold, sterile environment of the hospital room. Their argument, which had started as a whisper, soon became a roaring storm.

Mylan's eyes bore into Nora's with a fury she had seldom seen. "So all this time, you lied to my face?"

Nora's defensive posture matched her words. "Shut up, Mylan! I'm so done with you right now."

"Sage is angry with you, not because of Henry's death, but because she discovered you orchestrated it!" Mylan's voice cracked.

"How dare you even insinuate that!" Nora spat back.

Before either could continue, the door clicked and swung open, and revealed a middle-aged nurse with an air of authority. Her crisp white uniform contrasted with the colorful badge of her ID card and pins on her chest. Her eyes, although weary of what might have been a long shift, bore into both of them with a no-nonsense stare. "Keep your voices down or I'll have no choice but to ask you to leave," she said, her tone leaving no room for argument. As quickly as she appeared, she was gone.

Returning his attention to Nora, Mylan's voice dropped to a growl. "I tried to protect you. I moved you to Buffalo, away from all of this. But you brought trouble with you, didn't you?"

Nora's response was swift. Her eyes shimmered with barely held back tears. "You dragged me into this life! Now you're mad because I've taken control of it?"

Mylan expressed disappointment at her response. "You're still that same immature girl. Grow up, Nora. You never think about anyone but yourself, do you? Did you even consider Sage or Avery? Did you". "You're still that same immature girl. Grow up, Nora. You never think about anyone but yourself, do you? Did you even consider Sage or Avery? Did you think about them when you got into this mess?"

"I am doing what's best for me and my kids. Right now, they need to stay with you," Nora snapped back.

As Mylan prepared to counter, a soft rustling cut him off. Sage's fingers twitched, her eyes fluttered open, bringing a sudden silence to the room.

"Sage!" Nora said, tears formed in her eyes. "Oh my god, thank God you're okay."

Disoriented, Sage tried to focus on the faces hovered above her. "What happened? Where am I?" she asked, grimacing as pain shot through her body when she tried to sit up.

Nora, desperate for answers and perhaps a sense of vengeance, leaned in closer. "Who did this to you?"

Hesitation filled Sage's eyes. She recalled the attack, the faces, the laughter, the pain. "Why do you care?" she whispered, her gaze drifted away.

"The police will be here soon," Mylan interjected, his voice gentler now, filled with concern. "You need to tell them what happened."

Sage's resolve hardened. "I'm not talking to the police," she said. "I'll handle this my way."

The atmosphere in the room shifted from tense to heavy. The dull hum of the hospital's HVAC system was the only consistent sound, creating a backdrop to their strained conversation.

"Sage, these streets will chew you up and swallow you alive. This is not something you handle on your own," Nora's voice echoed as she looked at her bruised daughter.

Mylan stood near the window with the soft city lights painted a gentle glow behind him. "As much as you don't want to hear this, it's the truth. If you go out seeking revenge, they'll find your..." He paused, took a deep breath, "Your body will be floating somewhere in Coney Island beach."

A glimmer of defiance sparked in Sage's eyes. "At least I will be with my father."

Before they could say any more, the door opened with a soft click. Two detectives entered the room. Detective Douglas was tall, with a bald pate and a stern yet concerned expression. Detective Matthew was shorter, stockier, with a full head of graying hair, and eyes that missed nothing.

Sage instinctively pulled the blanket up, her body language becoming defensive and closed off. Her eyes darted between the detectives.

Nora, being the bridge between the law and her daughter, and offered a comforting smile, her posture straight. "Hello, I'm Nora Woods, Sage's mother."

Douglas nodded politely. "Sorry to interrupt. I'm Detective Douglas and this is Detective Matthew." He gestured towards his colleague. "We'd like to ask Sage a few questions."

Sage mustered enough strength to sit up slightly in bed, her fingers playing with the edge of her blanket.

"On the night in question, where were you coming from?" Detective Douglas asked, his tone professional.

"I went to a party on Long Island," Sage responded, her voice barely more than a whisper.

"Whose party was it?" Matthew interjected; his voice held an undertone of skepticism.

Sage hesitated; her nervousness clear as she avoided eye contact. "I don't know exactly whose party it was. Just a bunch of kids from school."

Matthew raised an eyebrow. "So, you went to a party, but you don't know who threw it?"

Mylan, protective and assertive, broke in, "Ain't that what she said?"

Detective Matthew shot him a look, his patience clearly thinning.

Douglas tried to steer the conversation back, "The girls that jumped you, have you ever seen them before?"

Sage's gaze shifted to Nora, searching her mother's eyes for guidance. "No, I've never seen them before."

"And would you recognize them if you saw them again?"

Sage hesitated, her body shrinking further into the bed. "I don't remember what they look like. It was really dark."

Frustration was evident on Detective Matthew's face, with deep forehead lines and knit eyebrows. "Well, what do you remember?" he pressed, his voice a shade more aggressive.

From the corner of the room, Mylan's face set in a hard expression. He moved forward, each step deliberate and menacing. "I won't tell you again," he growled.

The tension in the room grew thick, almost palpable. Matthew, sensing a potential altercation, bowed out. With a swift, sharp exhale, he turned on his heel and walked out, letting the door close a bit too forcefully behind him.

Detective Douglas took a moment to regroup before he continued. "Do you have any reason to believe that someone set you up?"

Sage tried to pull herself up. Her body ached with every movement. "Why would someone set me up? Nobody knows me," she murmured, her voice breaking.

Detective Douglas's eyes darted briefly towards Nora. "But people know me. Is that what you're getting at?" Nora's voice held a defensive edge.

Douglas shifted his weight from one foot to another, uncomfortable. "Do you have reason to believe that someone would target your family?" he directed the question back to Nora.

Nora's face flushed with frustration. "I could name a million people who'd want to harm my family, but what am I supposed to do? Keep my kids hidden away, pull them out of school?" Her tone dripped with sarcasm.

Douglas's stance changed slightly. He crossed his arms over his chest, the stern facade slipping. "As of right now, we have little evidence. Since Sage couldn't identify her attackers, our hands are tied."

Nora's desperation was evident as she asked, "What about stationing a police car outside her school?"

Mylan interjected, his voice firm. "There's no need for that. I'll be handling Sage and Avery's transportation to and from school."

Douglas nodded slowly and turned his gaze to Sage. "Sage, if anything comes back to you, please give me a call." He extended his business card, which she took gingerly. "And I apologize for my partner's behavior," he added.

As the door closed behind Douglas, Mylan moved swiftly to ensure it clicked shut. "I can arrange protection for both Sage and Avery. We don't need to involve the police further."

Chapter 6

Second Chances

Nora was in her new apartment kitchen, bustling about. As the coffee brewed, the aroma mixed with the scent of freshly cooked eggs and bacon in the air.. The sun streamed in through the window, as it highlighted the sporadic unpacked boxes and miscellaneous items scattered about. Although the scattered boxes and miscellaneous items suggested she wasn't fully settled yet, the open spaces promised a fresh start.

The unexpected knock at the door halted Nora in her tracks. Tension etched on her face, she quickly reached under the table, peeled off a gun taped securely to the underside. With practiced ease and stealth, she approached the door, her every sense on high alert. Glanced through the peephole, her face twisted in confusion when she saw nothing — someone deliberately covered it from the outside.

"Who is it?" Nora demanded, her voice a guarded growl. Only silence answered her.

With a determined exhale, she swung the door open, gun thrust forward, finger hovered over the trigger. But instead of a threat, she found Mylan, his hands raised in quick surrender, a few envelopes clutched in his grasp. "Woah, relax! It's just me," Mylan exclaimed.

"Why the hell didn't you answer?" Nora grumbled, as she set the gun down on the kitchen table before she returned to her culinary tasks.

Mylan smirked as he tossed the mail onto the table. "Got this for you. It was downstairs." He glanced around, admiration in his eyes. "This is a nice spot."

Nora chuckled softly and flipped a pancake. "Got a good deal. $1,500 a month."

He whistled. "For a two-bedroom in New York? Did you threaten the landlord or something?"

Nora grinned, "I have my ways, but uh, sorry about what happened at the hospital. That wasn't fair to you."

Mylan raised an eyebrow. "An apology from Nora Woods? Let me mark this day on my calendar." He laughed as he accepted the plate she handed him. "It's all good."

He chewed for a moment before he spoke. "I found a job for you. Security guard at a check-cashing place."

She almost choked on her coffee. "You're joking, right? I was the top homicide detective in my precinct, and you want me guarding checks?"

His gaze met hers. "And you're a murderer."

"Allegedly," she retorted.

Mylan sighed, pushing his plate away. "Look, you're not exactly everyone's first choice right now. This is the best I could find. Or there's a casino in Queens that needs security."

Nora, her pride stinging, reluctantly agreed. "Fine. The casino it is."

Mylan handed her a business card. "The owner owes me a favor. Don't mess this up. And if you see something... unusual? Turn a blind eye."

She took the card and met his gaze. "Got it." The unspoken understanding between them was clear. This job was more than just a second chance. It was a lifeline.

* * *

The sudden cascade of cold water shattered the early morning silence on Warren's body. He spluttered and jerked up from his once comfortable slumber, blinked rapidly as droplets slid down his face. "Ma, what's wrong with you?" Warren yelled.

Paulette stood beside the bed, her stance strong and challenging, an empty pitcher in her hand. "Get your ass up out of this bed," she snapped. The light from the room's single window cast a luminous glow on her stern features. "Lying here day in, day out. You made your bed, Warren, now you have to lay in it. And by that, I don't mean wasting your days away."

He rubbed his eyes and pushed the damp sheets off him and rose from the bed. His steps were heavy and weighed down as he made his way to the kitchen. The soft pad of his feet on the tiled floor and the ruffling of his disheveled pajamas were the only sounds that accompanied him. He pulled out a stool at the counter and rested his head on his arms.

His mother wasn't far behind. She leaned on the opposite counter. "Your probation officer called. Did you think I wouldn't know about your lax attitude towards finding a job?"

Warren mumbled, feeling defeated, "Nobody's hiring felons."

Paulette's voice grew intense, her words pointed, "You got a second chance, Warren. You came so close to being locked up for life. Donny and Sage, they saved you. Don't you dare waste this opportunity."

Warren looked up, his face a canvas of regret. "I'll find something."

Paulette pondered for a moment, "As much as I don't like him, doesn't Trigger run a mechanic shop? Might be worth asking him."

Warren hesitated and ran a hand through his damp hair. "I don't know, Ma. Maybe I'm not cut out for this. Maybe they're right about me."

Paulette's heart ached at the resignation in her son's voice, but she wouldn't let him spiral. Not now, not after everything. "If you want to change the narrative, Warren, start with your actions. So that means you can't kill, kidnap, and then complain about how people view you. Pick a struggle."

He let out a short laugh, surprised by his mother's sharp wit, "You right, Ma." He leaned back in his seat and picked through a small stack of mail that had been pushed to the side of the counter.

A chime from the doorbell interrupted the atmosphere, which caused Warren to glance up briefly, a letter still in hand. Paulette pushed herself off the counter and approached the door, opening it to reveal Donny.

Warren's body immediately tensed, his jaw clenched as he recognized the figure. "Why are you in my house?" His voice was hard, accusatory.

"Excuse me," Paulette interjected sternly, "You mean my house. And don't you start with that. Donny is your family, and he did you a solid."

Warren's eyes flashed, "He ain't family. I don't fuck with stitches."

Donny stepped further inside, a weariness in his eyes, "Warren, you can be mad all you want. But if I hadn't spoken up, things would've turned out differently for both of us."

Warren's gaze was steely, "Should've kept your mouth shut."

Donny tried to keep his calm, straightened his posture, "Man, you're always on me about school, about staying on the straight path. When I finally make a choice that protects my future, you get pissed?"

Paulette attempted to mediate and approached her son. She placed a gentle hand on his arm. "Sometimes, to be that better person, you have to let go of old grudges, baby."

Warren exhaled sharply. His eyes never left Donny's. Without another word, he scooped up the rest of his mail and headed towards his room and shut the door firmly behind him.

Donny, clearly affected by the confrontation, ran a hand over his face. Paulette approached him, "Don't worry about him. He's hurting, and he's healing. Give it time."

With a nod, Donny moved to hug Paulette, a simple gesture of gratitude. She held him close for a moment before he pulled away and left, leaving the room filled with the heavy weight of unsaid words.

Chapter 7

Bonds Tested

Sage sat uncomfortably close to the pastel walls and motivational plaques in Ms. Collen's cozy office. Ms. Collen's desk was uncluttered, save for a few stacks of papers and a photograph of her with a golden retriever. The soft hum of the air conditioner was the only sound between their exchanges.

"I just want to welcome you back to school. I know this past month has been hard for you," Ms. Collen began, her tone warm as she tried to break through Sage's emotional barriers.

Sage shifted in her seat and looked everywhere but directly at Ms. Collen. She clenched her jaw and curled her hands into fists, as if she physically held back the torrent of emotions that built up inside her.

"Would you like to talk about what happened?" Ms. Collen asked gently as she attempted to navigate the minefield of Sage's trauma.

"No," Sage shot back, her voice sharp as a blade.

Ms. Collen nodded slowly, her hands steepled in front of her as she chose her words carefully. "The last time we spoke, you mentioned your father's passing."

"Someone murdered him," Sage interjected bitterly.

The weight of that admission hung heavy in the room. Ms. Collen exhaled softly. "How does that make you feel?"

Sage's eyes flicked up, a storm of rage in them. "How does that make me feel? Are you serious?" She leaned forward, her voice trembled with barely suppressed rage. "I'm angry... I wish."

Ms. Collen waited patiently, her demeanor compassionate. "What do you wish?"

Sage's eyes glistened. A tear escaped. "I wish they had killed me, too. Anything would be better than this pain."

Ms. Collen's heart ached for the young girl in front of her. "Are you having thoughts of harming yourself?"

A scoff escaped Sage's lips, "If you think I'm going to do something to myself, don't. I'm not." She paused, her anger deflated, "Can we just end this session?"

"Before you go." Ms. Collen opened a drawer and retrieved two dice. With a soft smile, she handed them to Sage. "It's okay to feel anger or sadness. When you do, roll these dice. Allow yourself the number of minutes it shows to feel that way. No more, no less."

Sage held the dice and rolled them in her hand. "And when the time runs out?"

Ms. Collen smiled, her eyes kind. "Then find something, anything, that brings you joy, even if it's just for a moment."

Sage stood at her locker. The rhythmic thud of textbooks hit metal and echoed faintly. She'd organized her locker with meticulous care; photos of better times pinned up, post-it notes with reminders, and a small mirror. It was a small slice of personal space in an otherwise chaotic world.

As she rearranged her binders, she felt a presence approach. She looked up, her eyes met Tegan's. Following Tegan was Cylus, his tall frame slightly slouched and his hands shoved into his pockets, a look of genuine concern on his face.

Tegan wasted no time and pulled Sage into a tight hug. "Oh my god, are you okay?" Her voice was thick with emotion.

She pulled back but kept her hands on Sage's shoulders. Tegan searched her friend's eyes for any sign of lasting trauma. Nearby, Cylus shifted from foot to foot, as he didn't want to interrupt the moment but still wanted to show his concern.

"I'm sorry about what happened," Cylus blurted out, his voice earnest. "Do you know the girls that did it?"

Sage sighed and shook her head. "Thanks for your concern, but I'm okay. And no, I don't know who they were."

Tegan's eyes welled up again, "I wish I'd been there for you. I'm so sorry."

Sage managed a small chuckle as she tried to lighten the mood. "Then both our asses would've gotten beaten up. But, don't worry about me. Everything's all good now."

Tegan felt the weight of the moment and realized that Cylus might want a private word with Sage. She squeezed Sage's hand and shot a knowing glance at Cylus. "I'll see you later," she said, her voice soft. With a brief wave, Tegan drifted away and left the two of them alone.

Cylus took a deep breath. "I know this is both our free period. Um..." he began and glanced at Sage with a hint of nervous anticipation. "Would you like to go to the Misty Beans Café? They've got this coffee blend called Pandora's Box," he added with a slight chuckle. He tried to infuse some levity into the atmosphere. Sage could see the effort he made and couldn't help but smile.

***

Sage and Cylus sat at a corner table at Misty Beans Café, a place where the clink of mugs and the soft hum of conversations meshed perfectly with the gentle plucks of an acoustic guitar being played in the background. A pair of mismatched mugs sat before them, steam dancing upwards as they cooled.

Sage glanced down at her cup and giggled, "I guess they call it Pandora's box because everything is popping out of it.

I mean, look at this," she said as she pointed to the coffee that was filled to the brim of her cup, close to spilling.

"All the secrets pop out of Pandora's box," Cylus remarked, as he mimicked an explosion with his hands.

She leaned in, a playful glint in her eyes. "How about you tell me a secret? Something nobody knows."

Cylus took a moment, "Uh, my mom is planning on running for governor."

Sage rolled her eyes and laughed, "I could Google that. Give me something juicy!"

Cylus hesitated for a moment and bit his lip, "Alright. Sometimes at street basketball games, I get a little kickback if I win or throw a game. Depends on the offer."

Sage's eyebrows shot up in surprise. "But you're rich!"

"Correction," he said as he tilted his chin up with mock arrogance, "My parents are rich. I'm not."

"Why jeopardize your future? What if your coach finds out?" Sage inquired as she leaned in with genuine concern, her fingers circled the rim of her coffee cup.

Cylus shrugged. "I like having my own money and he won't."

Sage leaned back, a smirk on her face, "Well, your secret's safe with me."

Cylus leaned in, the playful glint returned to his eyes. "Now, it's your turn. And make it juicy."

Sage took a deep breath, her smirk wide. "Well, my dad was killed, and then I found out he wasn't my real dad. My secret tops yours," she said with a chuckle.

Cylus's expression shifted, sympathy clouded his features. "That's... messed up."

She raised an eyebrow. "Don't be a party pooper. You're supposed to laugh."

He shook his head. "Trauma is not something I laugh about. I know what that feels like."

Sage's smirk faded, and she looked down, chastened. "I'm sorry if I made you uncomfortable."

He reached across the table and touched her hand gently. "Don't be sorry about how you cope." As he lifted his pinky, he proposed, "Let's pinky promise to never bring up our secrets to anyone but each other."

Sage nodded. Her smile returned as they interlocked pinkies and sealed their pact. Their eyes met, understanding passed between them.

As Sage and Cylus chatted, a natural connection grew between them. They laughed, shared stories, and found common ground, making the cafe around them fade into the background.

"Thanks for bringing me here," Sage said as she looked around the café. "It's calming, you know? A good place to just breathe."

Cylus nodded. "I come here often when I want to escape the pressures. High school, man, it's like another universe sometimes."

Sage chuckled. "True that. One filled with awkward dances, raging hormones, and mountains of homework."

"Oh, speaking of homework," Cylus began, his eyes wide, "Did you do that math assignment? Mrs. Rainer is going to kill me if I forget another one."

Sage groaned. "Math. Why did you remind me? Now I won't enjoy my coffee." She took a playful sip as she glared at him over the rim.

"I bet you're one of those 'A' students who finished it days ago," he accused, his tone playful.

"You'll never know." She winked.

They laughed, and Cylus was about to launch into another topic when he glanced at his wristwatch. His eyes widened. "Crap! We're gonna be late for the next period!"

Sage's eyes darted to her phone, her face paled. "Oh my god, we really lost track of time!"

As they rushed to gather their things, Sage knocked over her cup and spilled the last remnants of her coffee. Cylus grabbed napkins and helped her mop up the mess.

"Sorry," she murmured.

"No big deal. But we really need to dash!"

They two bolted out of the café, the bell above the door jingled in their wake. The barista at the counter was used to the high schoolers' antics and shook his head with an amused smile.

They ran together, their laughter echoed in the streets, their worries forgotten in their rush to make it back to school.

Amidst the hum of after-school chatter, Sage was about to leave the school grounds when she heard a familiar voice behind her.

"What's Up Bob?" Kamari teased, referencing Sage's current hairstyle.

The sun cast long shadows on the pavement as Sage turned to face her. A small smile curved her lips. "Hey Kamari."

Kamari stepped closer, her eyes narrowed at the sight of the healed bruise on Sage's face. She reached out and held Sage's chin to turn her face for a better look. "They got you good," she remarked, with a hint of concern in her eyes.

Sage felt exposed and pulled away as she rolled her eyes. The hint of frustration was clear in her voice. She countered, "I don't care. I'm over it, anyway."

Kamari's eyebrows knitted together, her tone incredulous. "Over it? They put you in the hospital. You need to go set it off like Vivica Fox."

Sage sighed. Her posture stiffened. "I can't do that."

A group of students walked past them, throwing curious glances their way, but Kamari's focus remained unyielding on Sage. "How'd you let them jump and rob you?"

Sage's eyes flashed, her voice sharpened, "I didn't let them do anything. And how do you know they robbed me?"

Kamari smirked. "The streets talk. Those same girls are by the park, bragging about it."

Sage's shoulders sagged, her voice a defeated whisper. "They cornered me. What was I supposed to do?"

Kamari's frustration bubbled over as she gave a soft shove to Sage's arm. "You fight back!"

A breeze rustled the leaves on the nearby trees, carrying the tension of their argument. Sage raised her voice, "I am not you, Kamari! I'm not some thug."

Kamari's expression darkened, the hurt evident in her eyes. "Is that what you think of me? That I'm a thug?"

Sage realized the sting of her words, replied, "I didn't mean it that way."

Kamari took a step back. Her voice shook with emotion. "I grew up with my grandmother. We didn't have anything. She was old and couldn't protect me. I had no choice but to defend myself. I may be a little rough around the edges, so if that makes me a thug, then so be it."

Before Sage could apologize, a voice interrupted them, "Everything okay, Sage?" It was Tegan, her brow furrowed in concern as she approached the duo.

Kamari's eyes shifted to Tegan before she settled back on Sage, her voice icy, "Don't come running when you need me." With that, she turned on her heel and strode away.

Tegan, trying to ease the tension, warned, "You should stay away from her. I see her in that park all the time. She's nothing but trouble."

The sun had sunk below the horizon. Sage felt a whirlwind, caught between the hurt from Kamari and the concern from Tegan. The weight of the day pressed down on her. She felt the urge to escape and find solitude.

Chapter 8

Temptation

The sun was setting, painting the Brooklyn skyline with shades of orange and purple. Mylan and Nora stood on the balcony of his condo. As they leaned against the railing, their silhouettes contrasted sharply against the backdrop of the descending sun.

The atmosphere was relaxed yet tinged with a hint of unease. Nora looked at Mylan. Her eyes reflected the golden hue of the setting sun. "I can't believe you're about to be a father. How do you feel?"

Mylan let out a short laugh and ran a hand through his hair. "All honesty, I'm scared as shit," he replied, a playful smirk on his face. "Being someone's father scares me. I did a lot of stupid shit in the past, and I would hate for someone to play with my child, and they end up in a ditch."

The gravity of his statement was met with a burst of laughter from both of them. The sound echoed in the evening air.

Nora shook her head in amusement, continued, "You've been doing such a great job with Sage and Avery. I know you'll be a good father. And, come on, everyone in Brooklyn knows not to mess with you."

Mylan looked thoughtful for a moment. "Speaking of Avery. Something's different about her."

Nora's eyebrows furrowed in confusion. "Different how?"

He paused, choosing his words carefully. "She comes home from school and goes straight to her room. Sometimes we don't see her until the next morning."

Nora sighed, her posture became slightly defensive. "She's almost thirteen. That's teenage girl shit. I went through it with Sage."

"I'm serious, Nora," Mylan pressed, concern clear in his voice. "Some days she won't even eat. You need to talk to her."

"I will," Nora said, her tone softened as she took in Mylan's earnest expression.

They shared a moment of silent contemplation as they looked out at the city. Breaking the silence, Nora added, "Speaking of concerns..." She hesitated. "You know, I start that security job at the casino next week. Just having my bare hands feels... insufficient. I'm thinking I need a gun."

Mylan's eyes widened. A hint of anger and concern flashed simultaneously. "Absolutely not. Last time you had a gun, bodies dropped. And if your parole officer sees you with it, you're screwed."

Nora's lips tightened, a mixture of annoyance and realization.

Mylan attempted to lighten the mood and suggested, "Sarah has a taser. Borrow it from her."

A smirk appeared on Nora's face. "By the time I dig that out of my pocket, it'll be too late."

The sound of the front door interrupted their laughter. Sage and Avery's voices echoed through the hallway. The two stepped inside from the balcony, welcomed by the familiar surroundings of Mylan's living space.

Avery, had hair pulled back in a loose ponytail, greeted them with a brief hug. Without uttering a word, she made her way past them and disappeared into her room.

As the warm Brooklyn sunset filtered through the sheer drapes of the balcony, Mylan and Nora had stepped into the condo. "Sage, come sit. We need to talk," Nora beckoned.

Mylan, Nora, and Sage settled onto the stools around the kitchen counter, an island of gleaming granite and stainless steel. The bright overhead lights illuminated the anxiety on their faces.

"I didn't do anything," Sage started defensively, her posture rigid, anticipating a lecture.

"It's not about anything you did," Nora replied, attempting to choose her words carefully. "Before I talk to Avery, I wanted to discuss something with you."

Sarah, sensed the gravity of the conversation, discreetly moved to the fridge. The low hum of the appliance provided a brief distraction as she pulled out a jug of water, giving the trio some privacy.

Nora took a deep breath. "Mylan and I–

Mylan cut her off, "Not Mylan, just you," emphasizing his wish not to be implicated in the decision.

Nora rolled her eyes. A hint of irritation flashed. "Fine. I was considering the idea of enrolling you and Avery in a private school."

Sage's eyes widened in surprise, her voice tinged with disbelief. "Another private school? Why? I hated the last one we went to upstate."

"I'm thinking of your safety. The current school just doesn't seem right," Nora stated, her voice firm.

Sage's agitation was evident. "Now, after everything, you want to think about our safety? Seriously, Nora? It sounds like an excuse."

"Sage! I am still your mother. Respect is essential," Nora fired back, her tone sharper.

Mylan sensed the escalating tension, intervened. "Let's take a step back and talk this through calmly."

Sage's voice quivered with emotion. "You just want to change our schools because you're scared someone's after you. I've made friends now. I can't start over again."

Nora leaned forward, eyes locked with Sage's. "This isn't a negotiation. I'm the adult, and you're the child. My decision is final."

The room was thick with tension, the earlier warmth replaced by a cold standoff.

Sarah had hesitated for a moment, gauging the tension in the room before bravely interjecting, "Maybe we can figure out a different solution where everyone gets what they want."

Nora's eyes had hardened, and she had turned sharply to Sarah. "No offense, Sarah, but this ain't none of your business." Her voice was bitter, and her posture had stiffened.

"Respect my wife!" Mylan's voice boomed, echoing slightly in the high-ceilinged condo.

Sage, with fire in her eyes, retorted, "Nora doesn't understand respect. She only thinks about herself. All this private school talk? It's because she knows if anything happens to me or Avery, she'll be the center of another media storm."

A tense silence had enveloped the room as Sage and Nora locked eyes. It was a silent battle of wills. Mylan tried to diffuse the tension, "This is what's going to happen. I'll assign one of my guys to watch over you and Avery, ensuring no harm comes to either of you. That way, everyone is satisfied."

As Mylan finished, Sage, her emotions boiled over, had spun on her heels and walked away. But before she could get far, Nora's hand shot out to grab Sage's arm in a tight grip. "Disrespect me again, and I will–

Sage, eyes blazing, interrupted her, "You'll what?" She whispered menacingly. "Kill me like you did my father? Just remember, karma is real, and you'll get everything that's coming to you."

With a swift jerk, Sage had pulled her arm free and stormed into her room. In a flurry of emotions, she had thrown her belongings haphazardly around the room. Her backpack landed with a thud, books and papers scattered. With a fierce kick, she had sent the hamper flying, clothes spilling everywhere. As she was about to hurl a pair of jeans into the growing mess, she paused. There was an unexpected weight in one of the pockets. Curiously, she reached in and pulled out...

Sage's hands trembled as she pulled out the bag of cocaine from the jeans pocket. The weight of the decision she was about to make was evident in her expression. She dropped the jeans in a heap on the floor and she strolled to her desk, her footsteps echoed her turmoil.

Sage's eyes landed on the Bible that Sarah had gifted her. It was a symbol of hope and redemption, yet in that moment, it became a stark canvas for her descent. She carefully emptied the bag, letting the cocaine cascade onto the bible's surface.

Beside it, the dice Ms. Colleen had given her. But to Sage, they symbolized chance and unpredictability. With a frustrated push, she sent the dice clattering onto the floor.

Taking a moment to steady herself, she bent down and took a tentative sniff of the cocaine. Her head jerked back at the potency of the drug, the sensation burning and overwhelming. Encouraged or perhaps desperate, she went for another, and then another, until the white powder vanished.

The next day, in the park, the rhythmic sound of dice rolled, and laughter echoed. Kamari and her crew were deep in a game. The stakes were evident. Sage broke their focus as she approached them with determined but uneven steps.. "I need to speak to you," Sage's voice, though shaky, was audible.

Kamari didn't look up, instead chuckled, "Office hours are closed."

Sage swallowed the lump in her throat, she persisted, "I... I want to be a part of your gang."

The laughter that erupted from Kamari and her friends was sharp and mocking. Sage's face turned beet red. The weight of their mockery pushed down on her.

Kamari, enjoying the discomfort, finally acknowledged her. "Get lost, schoolgirl."

"I'll do anything," Sage's voice wavered, but the desperation was evident.

Kamari motioned her friends away and focused her full attention on the younger girl. Gently, almost tenderly, she lifted Sage's chin with her index finger. "First, we don't beg. And as I recall, you called me a thug."

"I'm sorry," Sage murmured, "I didn't mean it."

Kamari leaned in, twirled a strand of Sage's hair around her finger. "But you did mean it. However, I see potential in you, a little sister vibe. So, tell me, what do you truly want?"

The words escaped Sage's lips almost in a whisper, "I want to release my pain."

Kamari leaned back, amusement in her eyes. "Then go to therapy. But if you want my help, you need to bring something substantial to the table."

Sage hesitated. Her emotions warred within her. But then, with a deep breath, she admitted, "I want... revenge."

A slow, wicked smile spread across Kamari's face. "Now, that's a language I speak fluently."

Chapter 9

Confrontation

In the dimly lit underground shooting range, the echoed pops of gunfire rang out, filling the air with a tense energy. Shooters were lined up in the crowded place, each deeply focused on their respective targets. Amidst this noise, Kamari led a visibly nervous Sage to an available lane.

Sage jumped, every fiber of her being rattled with each gunshot that rang out around her. Kamari's laugh, light and amused, broke through the tension, a stark contrast to the atmosphere. "Okay, we can use this one. Here, take this." Kamari extended a gun towards Sage, the metal sleek and cold in the dim lighting.

"How is this going to help me get back at the girls that jumped me?" Sage's voice carried confusion.

"I can't send you to a gunfight with no gun," Kamari replied, her tone matter-of-fact.

Sage's eyes widened. The gravity of the situation dawned on her. "I can't do this. Maybe I'm not built for this."

"Shut up and take the damn gun," Kamari ordered.

Sage's hands trembled as she reached out. The weight of the gun almost surprised her, causing her grip to falter momentarily.

"The most important thing you need to know," Kamari began, her voice stern, "Is if you pull out your gun, you better make damn sure you use it. Got that?"

Sage's head bobbed up and down, her anxiety was obvious. "How do I know if it's loaded?"

Kamari handed Sage an empty gun. "Feel the weight of it." The difference in heft was noticeable. "You feel the difference?"

Under Kamari's watchful eyes, Sage was given a crash course on aiming. "Be careful of the blowback," Kamari warned.

Taking a deep breath, Sage took her first shot. The bullet went wide, missing the target completely. Her face fell, the disappointment visible. Yet, before despair could settle, Kamari was beside her, whispering words of encouragement. "Remember now, slow... steady... squeeze."

With newfound determination, Sage took aim once more. This time, the bullet found its mark. A triumphant grin broke across her face. "I did it!"

"Good. Now do it again."

The weight of her actions hung heavily on Sage's shoulders. "I don't want to shoot anyone. I thought you would teach me how to fight," she admitted, her voice quivered.

Kamari swiftly took the gun from Sage's hands. Without hesitation or the use of ear or eye protection, she aimed and fired at the target, hitting it dead center. The deafening blast caught the attention of many in the range.

"I don't know what era you think we're living in," Kamari began, her voice dripped with condescension, "but you should always carry, especially if you're trying to get revenge on someone." She glanced sideways at Sage. "Fighting is easy, but it's harder to outrun a gun."

"It's illegal to carry in New York," Sage replied, a mix of defiance and concern noticeable in her tone.

Kamari leaned in closer, her gaze intense. "I'm happy you did your research. I'll make sure I tell your family that at your funeral."

The gravity of Kamari's words settled heavily on Sage. After a moment of reflection, her face hardened with resolve. "Give me the gun."

Kamari's lips curled into a sly, triumphant smile as she handed the firearm back to Sage, pleased with the transformation she was witnessing.

***

Kamari and Sage sat opposite each other at Belly Burger, a popular spot known for its juicy burgers and crispy fries. As they waited for their orders, the conversation drifted between past experiences and current challenges.

"You must have been living that suburban life in upstate if you ain't never touched a gun," Kamari remarked, munching on a fry.

"White picket fence and all," Sage laughed and her eyes twinkled.

Kamari leaned back, her face momentarily softened. "I hear that. Ain't nothing wrong with that. I've been living in Brooklyn my whole life, and I would give it up in a heartbeat to have that white picket fence. Every day the streets get more dangerous."

Sage's curiosity got the better of her. "Why were you living with your grandmother?" she ventured.

Kamari's expression shifted instantly. There was a guarded look in her eyes, one that hinted at a deep reservoir of pain. "Parents died when I was young. My grandmother was there to pick up the pieces."

Regretting her intrusive question, Sage quickly said, "I'm sorry I asked."

Kamari leaned forward, her voice firm but not unkind. "Lesson number two. Stop apologizing. Say what you mean and stand on that shit. That's how you get respect."

"I said what I said." Sage's voice carried a newfound confidence. Her posture mirrored her words.

"Exactly." Kamari extended her hand, and they exchanged a high-five.

Sitting amidst the bustling ambiance of Belly Burger, the two girls found themselves delving deeper into personal territories.

Kamari studied Sage, her head tilting to one side, as if trying to decipher a puzzle. "So what happened to that white picket fence?" she finally asked, her voice gentle but probing.

Sage hesitated. Her eyes dropped to her plate as she processed memories and emotions. "My father was murdered," she admitted softly, her voice barely above a whisper.

Kamari's eyebrows raised slightly. "And your mom?" she pressed on as she leaned forward.

Sage's fingers played with the napkin beside her plate. Choosing to distract herself, she took a slow bite of her burger before she answered. "Our relationship is... not the best right now."

Kamari leaned back. "Interesting," she mused, her gaze unwavering. For a moment, the two of them were surrounded by an invisible barrier, their personal stories and struggles laid bare between them.

As they continued to chat, Sage's expression turned contemplative. A soft smile played on her lips as she looked at Kamari.

"Why are you smiling at me?" Kamari asked, a hint of suspicion in her voice.

"It's just that..." Sage began, searching for the right words, "I've always been the big sister. Avery always looks up to me, but I never had a sister to look up to, until now. You're like the big sister I've always wanted."

Kamari, often so self-assured and dominant, seemed momentarily taken aback. There was an awkward pause, followed by a genuine, but uncomfortable smile. She may have been many things in her life, but being seen as a 'big sister' was unfamiliar territory for her.

* * *

The dim glow from the hallway light fell on Sage as she slowly opened the front door, trying to slip inside unnoticed. The room was quiet except for the soft humming of a refrigerator and the distant echo of a siren. But as Sage stepped further in, she realized she wasn't alone.

Mylan, Nora, and Sarah sat stiffly in the living room, their faces taut with worry and frustration. Their combined gaze was unsettlingly focused on Sage, who felt like a mouse caught in a trap.

"You better have a damn good reason why you ditched the driver that was supposed to bring you home right after school," Nora's voice was icy, demanding an answer.

Sage responded with a roll of her eyes. Her voice dripped with teenage nonchalance. "I was out with my friend."

Nora leaned forward, eyes narrowed. "What friend?"

"Someone you don't know," Sage replied dismissively.

The tension between the two escalated. Nora took a step towards Sage, irritation on her face. "I'm not in the mood for games," she said.

Sarah tried to mediate, her voice calm. "Let's not shout. We can talk about this."

Sage's defiance was clear. "What's there to discuss? I came home late. It is what it is."

But the deeper issues surfaced when Nora, in a bid to assert her authority, tried to physically confront Sage. Mylan quickly intervened, separating the two.

"Sage, we're just worried about you," Mylan tried to reason.

But Sage was having none of it. She locked eyes with Nora. "You lost the right to worry about me when Dad died."

Without waiting for a response, she continued with her bombshell, "Nora set my father up to be killed by Warren, who happens to be my real father. If it wasn't for her, dad would still be here."

The room went silent. Sarah looked at Nora, waiting for a denial, but none came. "Nora, is this true?"

Without warning, Nora's hand flew, landing a harsh slap on Sage's cheek. The impact left an angry red mark.

The sudden commotion drew Avery, who had been asleep. She stared in horror at the scene before her.

As Nora reached out to her younger daughter, pleading, "Baby, I can explain," Avery turned on her heels, fleeing to her room. The slam of her door echoed throughout the house.

Nora and Sage locked eyes, an unspoken challenge passed between them. Sage's voice was low, filled with menace. "I am going to make you regret taking our father away."

Chapter 10

Reckoning

Warren was lost in the morning's rhythm, flipping pancakes and the sizzle of bacon filling the air. The aroma hinted at a hearty breakfast. As he turned to check on the eggs, an unexpected knock rang out. With caution, Warren approached the door, unlocking and opening it to reveal Donny.

Donny didn't wait for an invitation, just stepped in. His eyes darted around. While Warren resumed his cooking, Donny spoke up, his tone somewhat strained. "Just grabbing some things. I'll be quick."

He disappeared into a room, and moments later emerged with a bag bulging with clothes. Donny seemed intent on a hasty exit, but Warren's offer halted him. "Hungry?"

Donny hesitated for a mere second before letting the door close behind him, settling into a chair. His posture was tired, worn out. "Been crashing at Triggers' place," he admitted.

Warren's eyebrows knitted together, concern apparent. "I've warned you about him."

Donny responded with frustration, saying, "You iced me out. Where else was I supposed to turn? I kept you out of jail, remember?"

Warren's voice took on a harder edge. "By turning informant."

Donny's face flushed, his defense immediate. "I did what I had to. Not just for me, but for you, too. Those street codes? They don't keep you safe or put money in your pocket when you're inside."

Warren ran a hand over his face, visibly conflicted. "All I wanted was revenge on Nora, to make her pay. But now? I'm out, and I have no plan, no future."

Donny leaned forward, the earnestness in his gaze unwavering. "Start over. Find a job, talk to someone about all that anger. And maybe... try speaking to your daughter."

Warren's face paled slightly at that last suggestion. "After everything? She wouldn't want to see me. Honestly? I wouldn't blame her."

Donny's eyebrows shot up. "You didn't know she was your daughter when you did it."

Warren rubbed the back of his neck, tension evident. "Ignorance doesn't excuse the hell I unleashed."

Donny looked thoughtful for a moment. "Yet she didn't stand up in court against you. Ever wonder why?"

Warren's eyes were heavy with a mix of guilt and confusion. "If she has even a fragment of her mother's spirit, she has her reasons."

Donny leaned closer, probing. "Speaking of Nora, heard from her?"

Warren's facial expression slightly contorted, betraying a tinge of resentment. "Nora's the last thing I want on my plate right now, especially with my parole officer constantly on my back."

"Well, look, I know you don't like him, but Trigger offered you a job if you need one," Donny said, trying to shift the mood.

Warren sighed deeply, eyes softened. "Donny, I owe you an apology. I've been seeing you as the young boy you once were, not the man you've become. Your choices, your life, it's not for me to judge."

Emotion charged the air as Donny rose and pulled Warren into a tight embrace. "I'm sorry for ratting out. Thought it was the right move."

Warren pulled back, his eyes earnest. "It was. My anger blinded me. I'll meet Trigger at his shop tomorrow."

As Warren began rifling through a drawer, Donny's curiosity piqued. "What are you looking for?"

Warren held up a piece of paper. "Therapist that mom mentioned. Said she operates over Zoom, or something like that. Might be time to give it a shot."

Donny's smile slowly expanded, revealing his apparent sense of pride.

* * *

Sage diligently practiced her basketball moves in the gym, focusing on her shots. As she went through the drills, Cylus entered, a curious expression on his face.

"How's the arm?" Cylus inquired.

"A little stiff, but I'll make it," Sage admitted, trying to flex it a bit.

Seeing her struggle, Cylus chuckled, "I heard you made the basketball team."

Sage smirked ruefully. "More like a sympathy spot. I'm the water girl until I get the green light from the coach."

Cylus laughed genuinely, making Sage playfully swat at him. The mood shifted slightly as he moved closer. Sensing his intent, Sage instinctively backed away as she created some distance between them.

Quickly covering the awkward moment, Cylus handed her a flyer. "There's a street basketball game this weekend. You should come."

Sage hesitated, "Cylus, I just-

But he cut her off, nodding in understanding. "No worries. Maybe I'll see you there."

Just then, Kamari entered the gym, confidently striding past Cylus. Not one to shy away, she blatantly remarked, "Damn you, fine."

Slightly taken aback, Sage shot back, "What are you doing here? How did you even get in?"

Kamari waved her concerns away. "Never mind that. We've got work to do."

Sage frowned. "We don't have a session today."

With a sly grin, Kamari held out a gun to Sage. "Lessons are over. Welcome to the real deal."

Sage's eyes widened, her palms sweaty. "I'm not ready. I need to train more."

Kamari's expression hardened. "This isn't optional. There's someone who owes me. Get my money, or we'll have issues."

***

The streetlights cast an ambient glow in the dim street, occasionally flickering, adding to the tension in the air. Kamari's car, a sleek black sedan, sat parked inconspicuously a little distance away from a dimly lit street corner.

Inside the car, Sage and Kamari were engaged in a hushed, intense conversation. Kamari, with her dominant presence, pointed towards a man.

"There he is. The flashy one. His name is Que. He owes me twenty-five thousand dollars. Tell him you came for Chuckie's money."

Sage's eyes darted in the direction Kamari pointed, then quickly back to Kamari. There was a heavy sense of apprehension in her voice that was unmistakable. "Who the hell is Chuckie?"

"Just do it," Kamari hollered with palpable impatience.

Sage took a deep breath as her mind raced, "What if he doesn't give it to me?"

Kamari's eyes darkened. "You get it by any means necessary."

Sage gulped. Her wide eyes reflected the inner turmoil and the weight of the situation.

Taking another deep breath, she slowly opened the car door, the slight creak sounding unbearably loud in the silent night. She hesitated for just a moment, then started walking towards the group of men. Her footsteps seemed to echo back to her, each step amplifying her heartbeats.

The three men, lounging casually, turned their attention to her as she approached. The silence grew heavier, the air thick with tension. "You lost, little girl?" the burliest of them, with a mocking smirk, questioned.

Sage paused and took another steadying breath. "I'm here to speak to Que," her voice just above a whisper.

From the middle of the group, a man with a flashy gold chain and a cocky demeanor stepped forward. "Who's asking?"

Sage, visibly shivering from a combination of cold and fear, replied, "I came for Chuckie's money."

Que scoffed, the amusement clear in his voice, "Chuckie will get her money when I'm good and ready. Get the fuck out of here, little girl, before you get yourself hurt."

But Sage, pressed on, her voice quivered, "I need that money right now."

Que's eyes narrowed, showing his displeasure. He took a threatening step closer to Sage, "Bit-

But before he could finish, Sage's reflexes kicked in. She quickly pulled out the gun and pointed it right under his chin, her voice sharp. "Give me the money, now."

Her hand shook, and the weight of the gun was foreign and unsettling.

Que recovered quickly, laughed. The sound echoed eerily in the night. "You ain't never shot someone before. I can see the fear in your eyes."

The charged air around them turned even more palpable, thickening with the weight of the confrontation. Sage's eyes, already widened with fear, now bore into Que with a hint of defiance.

"What's ya name?" Que asked, his voice dripped with amused mockery.

Sage tossed her head, her voice carrying a hint of bravado she didn't quite feel. "Why you need to know?"

Que threw his head back and laughed raucously. "I want to make sure they spell your name right on your tombstone."

Fighting the wave of terror threatening to drown her, Sage's voice trembled, "My name...is Sweetie."

Que raised an eyebrow, seeming a touch surprised by her answer. Trying to show a facade of reason, he offered, "Sweetie, if you put the gun down, I'll give you the money."

She hesitated just for a split second and slowly lowered the gun, her grip loosening.

That was all the opening Que needed. In a swift motion, his hand shot out, grabbing Sage firmly by the neck. As he tightened his grip, her face turned a shade of purple, her eyes bulging in terror. Gasping for breath, Sage choked out, "Let... me." She gags, struggling for air. "Go."

Without warning, a deafening BOOM shattered the night.

Que's eyes went wide, his grip around Sage's neck slackened as he crumpled to the ground. Blood pooled around a gunshot wound in his neck, glistening darkly under the dim light.

The surrounding atmosphere, already tense, erupted into chaos. The men who were with Que and other bystanders scattered in all directions, their figures disappeared into the shadows.

Sage stood rooted to the spot, shock painting her features pale. The harsh reality of the situation, the gunshot's deafening echo, and the weight of the life lost played in a loop in her mind.

Kamari, ever the opportunist, sprinted over. Without hesitation, she rummaged through Que's pockets, yanking out wads of cash. "Let's go right now," she commanded.

Yet Sage seemed trapped in her own world. She stared at the lifeless body; her face a canvas of horror, guilt, and disbelief.

"Sage, come on!" Kamari's frantic voice jolted her back to reality. Kamari grabbed Sage's arm, pulling her towards the car to flee the scene.

The car's interior was filled with the smell of leather and a heavy tension. Kamari's eyes gleamed with excitement as she said, "Oh my god. I can't believe you shot him. You did that shit."

Sage's stomach churned and twisted, causing a wave of nausea to wash over her. She felt a cold sweat break out on her forehead and her mouth watered, a sure sign that she was about to be sick. "Pull over," she said weakly. The gravity of her actions hit her all at once.

"Why?" Kamari shot a questioning glance her way.

"Pull the damn car over!" Sage's voice rose in desperation.

The tires screeched as Kamari pulled to the side. Sage flung open the door and doubled over, heaving onto the gravel. The sound of retching filled the night, mingling with the chirping of the crickets. When she finally straightened, her face was ashen, and her eyes filled with fear.

Kamari's face was etched with concern. "Are you okay?"

The weight of it all was too much for Sage. "Am I going to go to prison?"

Kamari barked a short, humorless laugh. "Calm down. You're not going to prison."

Sage's eyes brimmed with tears, her voice shaking. "I don't see the joke. I just killed someone, and the two guys with him saw my face." She paused, attempting to gather herself. "It was self-defense. I can go to the police and explain that. Right?"

Kamari leaned back in her seat, her expression turned serious. "You don't need to worry about those two guys. I have someone on it."

Fear danced in Sage's eyes. "What is that supposed to mean?"

Kamari shifted slightly, her body taut with irritation. "You know what your problem is? You ask too many damn questions." She exhaled, her demeanor softened. "Everything is being handled. You did your part. Let me do mine."

Sage's eyes widened with fear. Before she could respond, Kamari handed her a bag. "Put your clothes in this and put these on." She handed her a set of fresh clothes. "And the gun. I'll take care of it."

Sage's hands shook as she took the items. "Thank you," she murmured.

Kamari leaned over, tucking a strand of Sage's hair behind her ear. "I should thank you for getting my money." Her gaze held Sage's for a moment. "I'll always protect you, as long as you protect me."

Sage swallowed hard, a million thoughts raced through her mind, her face a painted with confusion, fear, and a hint of gratitude.

Chapter II

Resonance

The Onyx Sabre Casino was a place where opulence met dark allure. Gleaming black marble floors reflected the soft, golden light from chandeliers made of onyx and crystal. The sound of clinking chips and distant laughter filled the vast hall, interrupted only by the hypnotic hum of slot machines and the soft rustling of cards.

There were private gaming rooms around the edge of the room that were covered by velvet curtains. These rooms were for high-rollers and celebrities who wanted privacy. The aroma of aged whiskey and exotic perfumes pervaded the air.

Nora stood, ever alert, her guard's uniform designed to balance elegance with function. As she absorbed the surroundings, a man striding with confidence towards her caught her attention. Tall and well-built, Luke was the kind of man whose presence was felt long before he arrived.

His rugged Italian charm was evident in his sun-kissed skin and sharp features. Nora could feel an unexpected tug, an attraction she hadn't accounted for, especially not someone younger than her.

"Nora, is it?" The lilt of an Italian accent in Luke's voice gave his words an added charm.

Nora straightened, maintaining her professional facade. "Yes," she replied.

Luke announced, "I'm Luke." He extended his hand, which Nora regarded but didn't accept. Undeterred, he carried on, "The boss wants to see you."

This made her raise an eyebrow, her defense mechanisms kicking in. "About?"

"Better ask him," Luke said as he nodded towards the grand door at the far end of the casino. The very door that led to Harry Sagen's office.

Nora took a moment, then started towards the door. Her heart raced. She was very aware of Luke's gaze on her as she walked. The sensation was exciting.

With hesitant steps, Nora navigated the maze of gambling tables and plush lounge chairs, arriving at a grand door, polished to perfection. Before she could knock, the door opened to reveal an expansive office.

"Mr. Sagen, you wanted to see me?" she asked, her voice shaky.

Harry Sagen, a picture of matured Italian elegance, awaited her. Silver streaks ran through his otherwise dark hair, and his gaze was as sharp as it was assessing. He motioned for her to sit. His voice carried that unmistakable tone of authority.

Feeling a knot in her stomach, Nora started, "I'm sorry about being late today. I was having some car trouble. Won't happen again."

His face remained inscrutable, devoid of any emotion. "That's not what I called you in here for. You've been here for about a week now. I've been watching you."

Her eyes widened. "You have?"

With a brief nod, he continued, "I did this favor because of the respect I have for your brother, so I looked past your discretions." Nora shifted, the weight of her past discretions bearing down on her.

Before she could reply, Harry got straight to the point. "I have another job that might be of interest to you."

She leaned forward, curiosity clear in her posture. "What exactly is the position?"

At this, Harry signaled his assistant. The assistant brought forward a decanter of deep red wine and filled two glasses. The liquid shimmered with ruby reflections. "Have a drink with me. The Witching Hour has a sweet taste to it."

She took a sip, her taste buds enveloped by the wine's rich flavors. "It's good."

He smiled, pleased. "I knew you would like it. It's actually one of my favorites."

Growing restless, Nora placed the glass on the table, her focus back on the matter at hand. "What is the position?"

The change in Harry's face was evident. It darkened with a blend of pain and determination. "Someone recently killed my stepson. I want you to find the person who did it and bring them to me."

Nora couldn't help the chuckle that escaped her lips. The insanity of the situation dawned on her. "You can't be serious?" she said, her voice tainted with disbelief.

Harry Sagen rose from his seat. The deep lines on his face emphasized the weight of his authority, and his gaze never wavered from hers. "Nora," he began, his Italian accent deepened with his gravitas, "I've never been more serious about anything in my life." Pausing for emphasis, he added, "I can pay you triple what you're getting now. "

She felt overwhelmed and took a deep sip of her wine, letting the liquid courage soothe her frazzled nerves. "I appreciate the offer, Mr. Sagen, but I'm not the person for the job. I just want to come here, do my work, and keep my head down." Setting her glass back onto the table, the slight clang echoed in the tension-filled room, she added, "I respectfully decline the offer."

She made a move to stand, and within moments, they were standing face-to-face. The contrast was clear. Nora looked strong yet vulnerable in her guard uniform, while Harry gave off an aura of power and danger as the embodiment of Italian mob authority.

His voice was steady, and his movements deliberate, conveying a sense of calm. "You know, I made a promise to your brother, so your job is safe," he assured her. Then, his voice dropped an octave, a dark edge coloring his words. "But, if word of this conversation leaves this room..." He trailed off for a heartbeat, letting the threat linger, "You'll find yourself buried next to your husband."

A tense silence blanketed the room. Harry's gaze shifted to his assistant, who stood at the corner. "Escort Ms. Woods out," he ordered tersely.

As they led her out, the weight of the conversation pressed heavily on Nora's mind.

Nora wrestled with her car key, turning it repeatedly in the ignition, but her car stubbornly refused to start. She muttered curses under her breath. She popped open the car hood to see if she could discern the issue.

"Do you need any help?" a familiar voice, edged with a hint of amusement, came from a few cars over.

Nora glanced up to find Luke leaning against his own car as he watched her. "No, I got it," she replied.

But as she fumbled around, clearly out of her depth, Luke shook his head, starting his own car and readying to leave. Just as Nora was about to give up, she exclaimed in frustration, "Damn it!"

Hearing her frustration, Luke turned off his engine and walked over to Nora. Without waiting for her approval, he inspected under her car's hood. "Looks like your alternator is giving up. You won't be able to start the car with this."

"Damn it," Nora muttered under her breath.

Luke leaned against her car, closer to her than before. "How about I give you a lift home?"

Nora hesitated for a moment, then nodded. "Alright."

As they drove, the weight of the night's events hung in the air. "Thank you. I owe you one," she said, trying to lighten the mood.

Luke glanced over, his tone more serious. "Whatever he wants you to do, just do it."

Nora blinked in surprise. "Excuse me?"

"He's my uncle," Luke said as he exhaled, "And I've seen enough to know that refusing Harry isn't a good idea. It will make your life here a living nightmare."

A heavy silence settled between them. She wasn't sure how deep Luke's ties with his uncle ran, but his advice felt genuine.

"How do I know you didn't mess with my car? Just so you can take me home to kill me?"

Luke chuckled. His eyes briefly glanced at her before focusing back on the road. "If I wanted to take you out, there are easier ways than playing mechanic."

Nora raised an eyebrow. Her lips curved into a teasing smile. "Is that supposed to make me feel better?"

Luke smirked. "Well, I am taking you home safely, aren't I?"

She leaned back, studying him. "You know, you look pretty young to be involved with all of... this." She motioned, encompassing the mysterious world of Harry Sagen.

He shot her a sly grin. "Age ain't nothing but a number."

Nora laughed, her anxiety easing a little. "So, are you trying to say you're old enough to be dangerous but young enough to be fun?"

He chuckled, "I like the way you put that. Spot on."

As Luke pulled up to Nora's apartment. He put the car in park and before Nora could unbuckle her seatbelt; he was already out of the car, moving with a swift purpose to her door.

Opening it, he offered a hand to assist her out. The streetlight cast a gentle glow upon them, creating soft shadows on the ground. For a moment, their gazes locked, and an undeniable tension filled the space between them. Their closeness made the atmosphere electric, their breaths becoming the only sound in the still night.

"Goodnight," Nora murmured, her voice just above a whisper breaking the trance. "And thank you."

Luke's intense gaze softened, his lips curving into a hint of a smirk. "Anytime," he replied, his voice low and loaded with a promise of more nights like this one.

* * *

The sun beat down, casting hard shadows on the concrete court. The rhythmic bounce of basketballs and shouts of players and spectators filled the air. Sage and Tegan found a spot on one of the worn benches lining the court. Sage tried to adjust her posture to find some comfort in the rigid wood.

The court vibrated with energy. Cylus was in his element, weaving through players. His shoes screeched on the pavement with every swift move. His jersey clung to him, soaked with sweat, evidence of the game's intensity.

The sound of bodies colliding echoed throughout the court as the players aggressively drove to the basket. The sound of heavy breathing, mixed with occasional shouts of frustration or triumph, added to the atmosphere of fierce competition.

"Is it always that rough?" Sage asked, wincing as a player nearly elbowed another in the face.

Tegan nodded, her eyes never leaving the game. "Always. Sometimes they almost come to blows. This is the street, so there are no rules. You can push and shove, but the game must continue."

Without warning, something slammed into Cylus from behind, knocking him off balance. He stumbled, falling onto the unforgiving concrete. A collective gasp spread through the crowd. Time-out was called, and a few players gathered around Cylus, helping him to his feet.

From their spot, Sage and Tegan noticed a wiry, older man with a stern face lean in, whispering intensely into Cylus's ear. His brow furrowed, Cylus nodded, and the man stepped back, fading into the crowd.

The whistle blew, and the game resumed with heightened tension. The clock ticked down, the scores neck-and-neck. In the last seconds, the ball found its way into Cylus's hands. He took a deep breath, dribbled to his spot, and released the ball. As it swished through the net, his team erupted in joyous celebration.

Tegan and Sage jumped off the bench, running onto the court. Sage hesitated for a moment as she approached Cylus, their past interactions lingering like a silent specter between them.

Tegan sensed the tension, rolled her eyes. "Oh my god, just hug already!" she insisted.

The push was all they needed. Cylus and Sage moved into a hug. It felt like time had rewound, a comfort reminiscent of old times. "Congrats on the win," Sage whispered.

Cylus pulled back, his eyes locked onto Sage's. "Thanks for coming. I guess I could call you my good luck charm."

Their eyes locked in a gaze that conveyed a depth of unspoken feelings and thoughts. Tegan, caught between the moment, made a face. "Ew, you two, get a room!" she teased, pulling them back to reality.

The celebratory atmosphere had cooled down when an unfamiliar weight wrapped around Sage's neck. Startled, she turned to find Kamari. Her dark eyes shined with mischief, her arm draped over Sage's shoulder. "Sweetie," she purred, "I didn't expect to see you here. Why don't you introduce me to your friends?"

Sage's eyes widened; she felt rigid under Kamari's grip. "Kamari, these are my friends, Tegan and Cylus," she responded.

Kamari's gaze fell on Cylus, sizing him up. "You're about to be the next LeBron?" she snorted with mock enthusiasm. Then added sarcastically, "Yeah right. You're not even close."

Sage's face tightened. "What are you doing here?" she snapped, uncomfortable with Kamari's intrusion.

The tension was so thick, you could cut it with a knife. The playful atmosphere had soured. Tegan and Cylus exchanged glances, eyebrows raised in silent questions about this unexpected intruder.

"Do you mind?" Tegan interrupted, her voice dripped with disdain. "We were in the middle of something."

Kamari's smile faded as she looked at Tegan, her posture turned aggressive. Sage, sensing the brewing storm, tried to mediate. "Kamari, let's just—

"What? You too good for old friends now?" Kamari barked, drawing attention from the surrounding crowd.

Voices murmured in the background. A group of Cylus' supporters had gathered around to protect him. Among the gathering faces, one caught Sage's eye. A rush of memories and emotions washed over her.

"Donny," Sage whispered.

Their eyes met, and the world seemed to stop. The surrounding noise became a distant hum as Donny stepped forward, separating from the crowd.

Without a second thought, Sage bolted towards him, wrapping her arms around him. The reactions amongst them were varied—Cylus seemed puzzled, Tegan's eyes widened, and Kamari was filled with a blend of ire and envy.

Finally, Cylus, ever the voice of reason, broke the silence. "Y'all know each other?"

Sage hesitated and glanced up at Donny, searching for the right words. "Yes, he's my-

"Family," Donny finished for her, his voice filled with warmth and certainty.

Donny tilted his head towards Cylus, signaling him to leave. Not missing the cue, Tegan took Cylus's arm, and they left together, giving Sage and Donny some privacy.

An awkward silence enveloped the two of them, broken only by the distant sounds of the chatter. There was a tension, apparent yet familiar, the kind that comes when two people who shared a past face each other after some time apart.

"You seem-

"I'm-

They both began at once, then giggled, the frosty atmosphere between them beginning to soften. Sage gestured for Donny to continue, a gentle nod to give him the floor.

"You seem better," he said, studying her.

Sage hesitated, her shoulders drooped. "I wish I could say that," she admitted.

Donny's expression turned somber. "I know a lot has happened, and I'm sorry that I didn't do more to stop Bunky from..." he trailed off, the unsaid words heavy between them.

Sage changed the subject, unwilling to dig up the past at that moment. "Um, how's college life?" she asked, forcing a hint of brightness into her voice.

"I'm graduating this summer," Donny replied, grateful for the change in topic. "I got an internship at the police department."

Sage raised an eyebrow. A smirk played at her lips. "Why would you want to be a cop? You a snitch now?"

Donny looked taken aback. "Excuse me. I'm trying to better myself. Especially after everything that happened. I don't want that kind of life for myself."

Sage folded her arms. "You're trying to better yourself, but you're out here betting on street games. Be real with yourself. This is the only life you know."

Donny's face tightened. "What's your problem?"

Before he could continue, Kamari appeared, her voice dripped with fake sweetness. "What's your problem? Why are you messing with my homegirl, Donny?"

Donny turned towards her, showing his state of confusion. "Your homegirl? How do y'all even know each other?"

"We go way back, right Sweetie?" Kamari shot Sage a pointed look. "Anyway, I don't mean to interrupt, but I need to speak to my friend... alone."

Sage could feel Donny's reluctance as he prepared to leave. "Listen," he began, looking at Sage, "I'm here if you need someone to talk to."

The sincerity in his eyes warmed her, and Sage nodded, "Thanks, Donny."

As they exchanged numbers, the weight of their shared history and the promise of a rekindled connection lingered in the air between them.

The basketball court, once filled with the energetic noise of a street game, was now quiet. The sun's afterglow painted the worn-out hoops in shades of deep orange and crimson, and the distant hum of traffic whispered of the city beyond. A lone basketball rolled to a stop near a trash can, forgotten by its owner.

Sage's posture was rigid. Her eyes darted around as if looking for an escape. The tension in her body was notable, every muscle taut. She seemed like a cornered animal, uncertain whether to flee or fight.

"You've been ducking me?" Kamari's voice, dripped with a mix of playfulness and menace, sliced through the silence.

Sage took a deep breath, her shoulders sunk, her clenched hands revealing white knuckles. "Matter of fact, don't answer that because I know you have," Kamari continued, her voice silky. "This is the life you asked for and now that I gave it to you. It seems like you don't want it. "

"We killed someone," Sage whispered. The weight of the admission caused her eyes to glisten.

A smirk played on Kamari's lips. "We... I didn't kill anyone. That was all you." Her tone was mocked, her eyes darting around as if daring anyone nearby to challenge her version of events.

Sage's voice trembled. "I thought you said you would protect me."

The court's overhead light flickered momentarily, casting a brief shadow across the scene. The two of them stood out against the dimming backdrop.

"And I did," Kamari shot back, her voice took on a dangerous edge. "I got rid of everything, including the two guys that saw you. I did that for you and then you ignored me." Kamari leaned in, her face inches from Sage's. "I don't like being ignored, Sage."

"The only thing I wanted was to make those girls pay for jumping me," Sage said in a desperate tone.

Kamari's mood shifted, and she let out a high-pitched, giddy laugh, her enthusiasm in stark contrast to the weighty conversation. "That's the next stop on our revenge train." She clapped her hands together, her eyes shined with manic glee.

Sage took a step back, her voice firm. "I don't want to kill anyone else."

Kamari pouted and rolled her eyes theatrically. "Where's the fun in that?"

Chapter 12

Entangled

A small potted plant on the windowsill added a touch of greenery, contrasting the muted beige curtains in Ms. Collen's office.

"Sage, we haven't spoken in weeks. How are you?"

"I'm okay. Sorry I haven't been here. I made a new friend."

Ms. Collen's eyes lit up, her face breaking into a genuine smile. "That's wonderful to hear, Sage! Tell me, who is this new friend?"

"She isn't a student here and doesn't go to school. She's more like a mentor or a big sister to me."

Ms. Collen's initial excitement shifted subtly to a more cautious intrigue. She picked up her pen and opened her notebook, writing a few words. "How did you meet this friend?"

Sage hesitated. Her eyes darted to the painting on the wall. She crafted her story carefully. "We met at a coffee shop. Just a chance encounter."

As Sage spoke, Ms. Collen's pen moved rhythmically, jotting down notes. "Have you reconciled with your mother?"

Sage's face tightened, her eyes narrowed. "Why are you changing the subject when I'm talking about my friend? I don't want to talk about my mother."

"I apologize for changing the subject," Ms. Collen said gently. "Tell me more about your friend. Where does she live?"

"I don't know. I've never been to her house."

"And does she work anywhere?" Ms. Collen probed further.

"I'm not sure. She's mysterious. Sometimes she just appears out of nowhere. Almost like a ghost."

Ms. Collen frowned, "What do you know about this girl?"

"Her parents died when she was young, and she ended up living with her grandmother. She goes by the nickname 'Chuckie'."

Ms. Collen's eyebrows raised in surprise. "Chuckie? You mean the doll from the horror movies?"

"You can't tell me what to do," Sage retorted, her tone defensive. "She's the only one who truly understands me. She makes me feel invincible."

Ms. Collen leaned forward, her tone softened. "I understand it feels good to have someone who understands you. But always be cautious."

Sage's eyes shimmered with unshed tears. "You're just like everyone else. Always judging."

Ms. Collen tried to redirect the conversation. "Have you tried using the dice coping skill I taught you?"

Sage sighed. "No, I keep forgetting. Can I go now?"

Ms. Collen nodded. "Of course. Just remember, sometimes forgiveness can heal wounds better than revenge."

With that, Sage turned on her heel and exited the room, leaving Ms. Collen in a contemplative silence.

* * *

Kamari looked over at Sage with a mischievous glint in her eye. "You know what we should do today?" she said, a sly smile playing on her lips.

Sage raised an eyebrow. "What's that?"

"We are getting you tatted," Kamari said, grinning. "You can't hang out with me with bare skin."

Sage's eyes widened in surprise. "A tattoo? Really?"

As they made their way to the tattoo parlor, Sage couldn't help but feel a sense of nervous anticipation. She had never gotten a tattoo before, but Kamari was there to reassure her, holding her hand as they entered the parlor and approached the tattoo artist.

"What are you thinking about getting?" Kamari asked.

Sage explained she wanted a tattoo on her inner wrist that said "Sweetie,"

As the tattoo artist inked the design onto her skin, Sage felt a mixture of pain and exhilaration, the buzzing of the needle sending shivers down her spine.

When it was finished, Kamari grinned. "That's fire!" she exclaimed.

***

Sage nervously followed Kamari through the dimly lit streets of the city, her heart pounding with excitement and fear. Kamari's wild spirit was infectious, and Sage couldn't resist the allure of her rebelliousness.

"So, where are we headed next?" Sage asked, trying to sound nonchalant.

Kamari turned to her with a smirk. "I'm headed to this abandoned warehouse on 5th street. You down to ride?"

The unknown thrill was too tempting for Sage to resist, despite the hesitation. "I'm with it."

It was eerie and unsettling, with broken windows and rusted metal fences lining the abandoned warehouse. Sage shuddered as she followed Kamari through the dark, musty corridors.

Sage was shocked to see a figure tied to a chair in the middle of the room. She gasped in horror as she realized a girl gagged and blindfolded, with her hands and feet bound tightly to the chair.

Sage was paralyzed with fear, unable to grasp the gravity of the situation. This was a novel sight for her, caused questions and fears to flood her mind.

Kamari pulled out a gun and handed it to Sage. "This is an early birthday gift."

"I can't do this Kamari. The first time was the last time. I'm not a killer."

Kamari's irritation simmered as she watched Sage hesitate, her hands shaking and her breath coming in quick gasps. They were in a dangerous situation, and Kamari needed Sage to get her shit together. "For God's sake, Sage, get yourself under control!" Kamari hissed, her voice laced with frustration. "If you did it once. Then you can do it again."

Sage's hand quivered as she reluctantly took the gun, feeling a sense of both shock and disgust.

Kamari leaned in closer, her voice dropped to a whisper. "This is one of the girls that jumped you. They put you in a hospital bed. Are you really going to let her get away with it?"

Kamari removed the blindfold, revealing a tear-stained face staring back at her. Her lips curled into a sinister smile as she stared back at the girl. Kamari glanced at Sage. "This is your opportunity. Get your lick back."

Kamari's eyes gleamed with an almost evil light, savoring the chaos she caused. She pointed to the girls' temple. "Shoot her," Kamari said with force.

Sage hesitated for a moment, her mind raced with doubts and fears. But something about Kamari's tone and energy was interesting, drawing her in like a magnet. "Okay." Sage steadily lifted the gun until it was directed at the head of the girl.

Sage's finger hovered over the trigger before she pulled. The force of the bullet knocked the chair down. The blood quickly ran out onto the ground.

Kamari smirked. "That's what I'm talking about. Let these bitches know. Sweetie is not to be played."

Sage's heart pounded with adrenaline as she looked down at the dead body in front of her. For a moment, she couldn't believe what she had done again, but as the realization sunk in, she felt a surge of satisfaction wash over her.

Chapter 13

Web of Deceit

Sage and Kamari were perched on a bench, sharing a joint. Their laughter was infectious, carrying across the park and attracting the attention of others. They continued to laugh when they saw Tegan approaching them. As Tegan got closer, Sage's smile faded, and Kamari's expression turned cold.

"Hey, Sage, what's up?" Tegan said as she smiled.

"I'm cooling. What's up?" Sage said, as she blew smoke.

Tegan waved the smoke out of her face. "I thought you would want to attend Cylus's game together. It starts in an hour."

"Oh shit. I forgot about that." Sage looked at Kamari for a moment, without speaking, communicated with her friend. Kamari's expression remained stern, and Sage turned back to Tegan, her voice firm. "On second thought, I'm not. Kamari and I have plans," Sage said, her tone polite but unwavering. "Have fun."

Tegan's face fell as soon as she realized Sage wasn't interested in going to the game with her. Her smile faded, and her expression turned crestfallen. "Oh, okay. I guess I'll tell him you had a family emergency," she said before turning to leave.

"She is such a lame. I don't know why you're friends with her," Kamari whispered.

Sage's eyes followed Tegan as she walked away. She felt a pit in her stomach as she watched Tegan's figure grow smaller and smaller, until she disappeared around a corner, out of sight. "I don't know either."

"I know you like Cylus. If you want to go to the game, then go. I'm not going to stop you," Kamari said.

"Nah, I'm good. What we should talk about is why I never see you with any guys," Sage laughed.

"I don't do boyfriends, but there is a guy that I'm interested in. His name is Donny. Remember you were talking to him at the basketball game that night?"

The sound of Donny's name caused Sage's heart to pound. Her hands clammed up, and she twisted them together in her lap. "Yea, I remember him."

"He said that y'all were family, but I've never heard you talk about him."

Sage took a deep breath. "He is my father's cousin," she paused. "My real father."

"I don't understand."

"I was raised by my dad, but I later found out that my real father was Warren. Warren Lafayette."

Kamari sat frozen in her seat, her eyes wide with shock. Slowly, Kamari stood up from her seat and looked at Sage. "I heard Mercy and Warren had a kid together but I didn't know it was you."

"She goes by Nora Woods now. How do you even know of her?"

"You're the daughter of Mercy Copper! She's like a living legend in Brooklyn. Her and Warren took down a kingpin back in the day. That's some gangster shit.

"Warren did a 15 year bid and missed out on college. I don't see the gangster in that."

Kamari's eyes darted upward. "College isn't all that it's cracked up to be. I think he went out like a G."

"That's not the life I want for myself."

Kamari turned to Sage with a steely expression, her eyes locked onto Sage's. "Don't forget your plan," she said firmly, her voice low and intense.

Sage nodded, a flicker of uncertainty crossing her face. She knew Kamari was referring to their plan for revenge, and the thought made her uneasy.

Kamari's eyes bored into Sage's, as if willing her to remember their pact. "We can't let them get away with what they did to you," Kamari continued, her voice rising in intensity.

Sage swallowed hard, feeling a knot form in her stomach. She knew Kamari was right, but the thought of revenge made her uneasy. She wondered if there was another way, a way to move forward without causing harm to others. "Everything that we've been doing hasn't made me feel any better. Actually, I feel worse. Forgiveness doesn't sound so bad after all."

Kamari's expression grew dark as she turned to face Sage. "Forgiveness is for the weak," she said, her voice dripping with contempt.

Sage felt a wave of unease wash over her. Kamari's words felt like a slap in the face.

"But forgiveness is important. I read in this bible my aunt gave me," Sage protested, her voice soft and uncertain. "It's a way to move on and let go of the past."

Kamari shook her head, her eyes flashing with anger. "No," she said firmly. "Forgiveness is just a way for people to avoid dealing with the truth. It's a way to make themselves feel better, without ever taking responsibility for their actions. Revenge is a way to hold people accountable for their actions and make them pay for what they've done."

Sage looked at Kamari with a steel determination in her eyes. "You're right," she said firmly. "Revenge is the only way to make them pay."

Kamari's eyes widened in surprise and then narrowed in satisfaction. "I knew you'd come around," she said, a hint of a smile playing at the corner of her mouth.

* * *

The sound of slot machines and chatter of gamblers filled the air, but Nora remained focused on her task. She observed the crowds, looking for any signs of suspicious behavior. She stood tall in the middle of the bustling casino, her eyes scanning the crowds for any sign of trouble. Suddenly, Nora's walkie-talkie crackled to life, and she heard a call for her to report to Harry's office.

As Nora made her way down the hallway towards Harry's office, she felt a sense of nervousness creeping up on her. She remembered Luke's advice about doing whatever Harry asked her to do or there would be consequences, and she took a deep breath to steady her nerves.

As she approached the door, she noticed that her heart was pounding in her chest. She took another deep breath and knocked. When Harry called out for her to come in, she opened the door and stepped inside.

Harry gestured for her to have a seat. "I just wanted to apologize for our last meeting. I know you have been through a lot and I would hate to be another problem in your life."

Nora felt the tension in her body dissipate. "No need for an apology. Thank you for understanding. I am just trying to make the right decisions in my life now."

Harry smiled. "I completely understand. I tried to help my stepson make the right decision and unfortunately, he wanted to make his own choices." Harry stood up from his chair and walked over to a picture of his stepson, a wistful expression on his face. He picked up the picture and cradled it, studying it for a moment before looking up at Nora.

"I loved that boy," he whispered, his voice heavy with emotion. "Just as much as you love your daughters. It's Sage and Avery, right?"

Nora's heart raced as she heard Harry mention her daughters' names. "Uh, yes. It's Sage and Avery," Nora replied, her voice hesitant. Nora's unease grew as Harry continued to hold the picture of his stepson and spoke again, his words heavy with implication.

"You'd probably do anything for them, huh?" Harry asked, his tone casual but with an underlying hint of menace.

"I'd do anything to protect the ones I love. And if that means taking matters into my own hands, then so be it. I did it once. I'll do it again," Nora said with conviction.

Harry placed the picture back on the table and sat in his chair. "That's what I like about you. You're not afraid to get your hands dirty."

"No disrespect, Harry, but where is this conversation going? I would like to get back to my post."

"The same way you would do anything for your girls. I would do anything to find out who killed my boy. You find out who killed him. I'll make sure your girls stay safe."

"If you touch a hair on my daughters' head. I will kill you."

Harry chuckled. "If you don't do what I say, you will be unemployed and your children will be dead."

Nora's emotions boiled over as she heard Harry's words, and without thinking, she lunged towards him. But before she could reach him, one of Harry's guards stepped forward and held her back, pinning her arms behind her back.

Nora struggled against the guard's hold, her heart pounding with anger and frustration. She could feel the adrenaline pumping through her veins, and she knew she had to get free.

"Get the hell off of me!" she shouted, her voice strained.

But the guard held her firm, his grip unyielding. Nora continued to struggle, her eyes fixed on Harry. "Nora, calm down," Harry said, his voice gentle. "I didn't mean to upset you. We're on the same team here."

She continued to fight against the guard's hold, desperate to break free.

"Let her go," Harry said firmly. "She's not a threat."

The guard hesitated for a moment, but then he released Nora's arms. She stumbled forward, her chest heaving with exertion. "I'm not doing shit for you. You son of a bitch."

Harry took a deep breath. "I don't think I made myself clear. There are no choices in this deal."

Before exiting the office, Nora turned to Harry and said, her voice cold and firm, "What is his name?"

"His name is Que," he said, his eyes fixed on Nora's.

Chapter 14

Tangled

The room was dully lit by the last light of dusk filtering in through the sheer curtains, casting a bluish tint over everything. The modest kitchen, with its mahogany cabinets and granite countertops, had never felt so heavy with tension. A barely touched plate of food sat on the counter, its warmth long gone.

"He was explicit in his orders; he wants me to handle it. I can't afford to put you in the crosshairs with him," Nora said, her voice thick with emotion. The strain in her eyes hinted at the internal battle she was facing.

Across from her, Luke leaned on the marble kitchen island, his frame cast a tall shadow. "I always knew he had a dark streak, but threatening your children? That's a whole new level of twisted," he muttered.

She drew her knees to her chest. Nora sat curled up in one of the high-backed chairs, looking small and defeated. "It's a no-win situation, Luke. If I bow down to his demands, I'm back in the mess I fought so hard to leave. If I resist, my kids- her voice broke, unable to finish the thought.

With a few steps, Luke was by her side, pulling up another chair to sit close, their knees almost touching. "What if I could mediate? Talk some sense into him, or at least buy you some-time?"

She looked up, a glimmer of hope in her eyes, then changed the subject slightly. "I know he's family to you, but what can you tell me about him?. What are his weaknesses? I need some-thing."

Luke hesitated for a moment, his gaze distant. Standing up, he wiped his brow with his forearm, a sign of his discomfort. "Veronica, his wife. But let me be clear, approaching her would be a suicide mission. I can't even get to her."

Nora's eyes narrowed with curiosity. "There's a story there. What went wrong between the two of you?"

He gave a half-smile. "You sure got time?"

In response, Nora reached into the cabinet above her, re-trieving a bottle of chilled Moscato. As she poured the golden liquid into two delicate glasses, she replied, "Right now? I have all the time in the world."

They clinked their glasses, breaking the heavy atmosphere and building a bond amidst the chaos.

Luke took the glass, rolling the liquid in it for a moment, lost in memories. "It started with my father, Russell. He and Harry, they had differences, but they were still family. Dad believed in partnership, trust, and respect. Harry believed in absolute power and domination."

Nora took a sip, her eyes fixed on Luke. She saw a vulnerability in him she hadn't noticed before. "So, Harry orchestrated a coup against your father?"

Luke nodded. "A debt was fabricated. An excuse to get my father out of the picture. It was a regular evening. Dad had a meeting, said he'd be back for dinner. He never made it home." A flash of pain crossed his eyes. "A week later, Harry paraded in, feigning sympathy. But behind that mask, I saw a predator. He gave me an ultimatum: work for him or follow in my father's footsteps."

Nora reached out and placed a comforting hand on Luke's. "And Veronica, Harry's wife?"

"She was my father's confidante. They were close friends even before she married Harry. There are rumors that Harry married her just to get closer to my father, to have an eye in his camp." Luke sipped his wine. "I tried to reach out to her once, hoping she'd help or at least shed some light on Harry's plans. But she's unreachable, guarded round the clock. She's untouchable."

They sat in silence, the weight of their problems pressing down on them. The evening wore on, the bottle emptied, and the distance between them closed. The troubles of the world seemed distant as the warmth of the wine and the electricity between them grew.

"I'm sorry you have to bear all this," Nora whispered.

"We all have our battles," he replied. Their faces were inches apart now, their breaths mingling.

"In this mess, you're the only silver lining," she murmured.

And just like that, the distance vanished. The intensity of their situation mixed with their growing attraction, pulled them into a heated embrace. Hours later, they found themselves wrapped in each other's arms, the concerns of the world momentarily forgotten as they lay together in bed, their souls intertwined.

The early morning rays bathed the room in a soft, golden glow, gently rousing Nora from her slumber. Her eyes fluttered open to find Luke's peaceful face beside her. He was still asleep, looking almost boyish in the morning light, a stark contrast to the assertive, protective man she had come to know.

Nora carefully extricated herself from Luke's embrace and slipped out of the bed. She tiptoed to the bathroom, freshened up, and slipped into her robe. When she returned, she found

Luke awake, propped up on one elbow, his eyes watching her intently. "Morning," she murmured as she offered a soft smile.

"Good morning," Luke replied, his voice husky. "Last night was... unexpected."

Nora took a deep breath, feeling the need to clarify things. "About last night... Luke, I didn't plan for that to happen."

He sat up and ran a hand through his disheveled hair. "Neither did I. But it did, and I don't regret it. Do you?"

She hesitated for a moment, choosing her words carefully. "Regret? No. But it complicates things. You're ten years younger than me, and in our world, that's more like a lifetime."

Luke's expression was pensive. "Age never mattered to me. I've been around people older than me all my life. But I get it. The last thing I want is for you to feel uncomfortable."

Nora sighed, her thoughts raced. "This isn't about age, not entirely. It's about me wanting to protect my heart. Things between us moved quickly, and I need time to process it all. I'm sure your uncle would not like this."

Luke's gaze was unwavering. "I don't care about him. Where does that leave us?"

She met his gaze head-on. "I value our connection, and I don't want to lose that. But I'm not sure I'm ready for a full-blown relationship."

Luke nodded slowly, "So, you're suggesting-

"Friends with benefits," Nora finished for him, a hint of nervousness in her voice. "At least for now, while we figure things out."

A slight smile tugged at the corners of Luke's mouth. "I'm open to it. On one condition."

Nora raised an eyebrow. "And that is?"

"That we keep communication open. If either of us feels differently or wants more, we talk about it."

Nora nodded in agreement. "Deal."

They both leaned in, sealing their new understanding with a gentle kiss. The uncertainties of the world outside their room might still loom large, but for now, they had found a shared understanding in each other's arms.

Chapter 15

Broken

The smell of grease and fresh rubber permeated the air inside the mechanic shop. Tools clattered against metal, engines hummed, and the sounds of distant laughter from the other mechanics could be heard. Warren, with sweat streaking down his dirt-streaked face, tightened bolts beneath a jacked-up car. His navy blue overalls bore patches of grease, a testament to the hard work he was putting in. The radio played a faint tune in the background.

The main entrance bell jingled, and a tall silhouette appeared. It was Donny, whose eyes scanned the shop before he landed on Warren, trying to wrestle with a stubborn bolt. "This is what I like to see. A working man," Donny declared with a chuckle, his tone light and teasing.

Warren slid out from beneath the car on his trolley, a grin breaking out on his face. Wiping his hands on a cloth, he stood and met Donny with a celebratory high five. "Man, what you doing here?"

"We need to talk about Sage. I ran into her at a street ball game the other day," Donny began, his jovial tone now replaced with one of concern.

The mention of his daughter caused Warren's cheerful demeanor to falter. His eyes tightened. "Why are you coming to me with this? It's not like I have control over where she hangs out."

"It's not about the game. She was with this chick named Chuckie. Trust me, she's bad news," Donny warned.

Throwing a wrench onto the worktable in frustration, Warren snapped, "If you're so concerned, call her mother. That's where Sage lives, not with me."

Donny's jaw tensed. The laid-back manner from earlier was gone. "She's your daughter too, Warren. And Nora should hear this from you. If something were to happen to Sage-

Warren's hands clenched, interrupting, "Sixteen years, Donny. I can't start playing daddy after sixteen years. After what I've done... How can I look at her?"

"Have you reached out to that therapist ma told you about?" Donny's voice softened, concern clear.

Sighing, Warren avoided Donny's gaze. "I've been doing better, especially since I started this job. Maybe I don't need therapy."

Donny's eyebrows knitted. "Trust me, you need it. More than you might think."

Warren's eyes darted away, a hint of resentment palpable as he fiddled with a tool.

"You know," Donny continued, "I think Sage might just be with Chuckie because she feels isolated. She probably thinks she doesn't have anyone else."

Warren shot him a skeptical glance. "Now you're playing therapist?"

Donny sighed. "What if I arranged a meeting for you and Nora? It's about time you both spoke."

Warren hesitated, his emotional walls faltered. "What's with this peace-making shit?"

"Life has a way of teaching you things. Everyone deserves a shot at redemption," Donny replied.

Warren sighed, rubbing his temples. "Alright. Set it up." Donny's effort to reconnect with a fragmented family had just begun.

* * *

The café had an air of nostalgia. Vintage posters adorned the walls, and the scent of fresh pastries and brewing coffee lingered in the air. The soft hum of conversations filled the room. Nora, dressed in a sleek blouse and jeans, sat on one end of a wooden booth, her posture rigid. On the opposite end was

Warren, in a neat pressed shirt, looking tense. Donny, ever the mediator, sat between them.

Upon seeing each other, their gazes locked. There was a tumultuous mix of emotions: anger, regret, pain, and somewhere deep down, a hint of the love that once was. The weight of their shared history was palpable.

Donny took a deep breath to break the silence. "I wanted to bring y'all together to make amends. Both of you made mistakes, and there's no reason we can't find common ground. Especially for Sage."

Nora's eyes flared, her voice raised in defensive. "What does Sage have to do with this? She's my daughter."

Warren swallowed hard, his voice a mere whisper, "Our... our daughter."

A bitter chuckle escaped Nora. "Did you raise her?"

Warren's face contorted as he struggled to keep his emotions in check. "You hid your pregnancy from me! How was I supposed to raise a child from behind bars? Or did you conveniently forget that part?"

Donny intervened, his voice firm but gentle. "This isn't why we're here. We're not here to argue."

Both Nora and Warren shot Donny a look. Their reactions, though stemming from different emotions, had the same underlying message: This was between them. Warren cleared his throat. "Donny, can you give us a moment?"

Understanding, Donny nodded and exited the booth, leaving Nora and Warren in an almost suffocating silence. They both fiddled with their respective drinkware, the clinking of cups the only noise between them.

Warren cleared his throat as he asked, "When did you find out you were pregnant?"

A deep, exhale escaped Nora. She hesitated, her voice softened, "A few days before. Before everything happened."

His voice cracked. "Why didn't you tell me?"

Nora looked down as she traced the patterns on the tablecloth, "I knew that if I told you, you'd have stayed in Brooklyn and given up on college. I didn't want you to one day look at me with regret, resenting me for the life you missed out on."

Warren's face contorted into a bitter smirk, the corners of his lips twitched with suppressed anger. "I resented you the moment those cuffs clicked on my wrists. Even if I had evaded prison, no college would've looked my way after that."

Nora's eyes shimmered. The weight of guilt pulled down the corners of her mouth, casting a shadow on her face. "What was I supposed to do? Stand by and let everything crumble? I was carrying our child and terrified out of my mind. I honestly thought we'd pull it off."

Warren's voice rose, strained with frustration. "That's the problem! You never stopped to think things through. I warned you not to go through with this plan."

She shot back, eyes fiery, "You weren't chained to me! You had every opportunity to back out. You chose to be there."

A tiny silver spoon, left abandoned beside a cold cup of coffee, glistened under the cafe's dim lights. It bore witness to their painful revelations, resting on the stained wooden table. Warren's face hardened, his voice dripped with accusation. "I was always there for you. Even when you made the stupidest decisions. But then, you killed my unborn child."

Nora's voice trembled, fighting back emotions. "Your child? What about the trauma you inflicted upon my girls? As for Isabella, I'm certain she's doing just fine."

Warren's expression turned to one of utter disbelief, the lines on his forehead deepened. His voice, soft yet intense, pierced through the air. "I traumatized your daughters? So planning and executing a man's death, their father's, was just a walk in the park for you?"

The silence that followed was thick, each person trapped in their own whirlpool of emotions, the weight of years of unspoken words pressed down upon them.

He spoke, voice choked with emotion, eyes threatened to spill tears. "I reached out to you from prison. Your mother told me you'd left Brooklyn. The anger... it consumed me." Warren's gaze met Nora's eyes, glistening. "But what tore me apart was the silence. Why didn't you call? Why didn't you ever come to see me?"

Nora's eyes brimmed with tears, threatening to fall. The weight of Warren's words pressed heavy on her heart. "It wasn't about you, Warren," she whispered as her voice trembled, as memories of the past resurfaced.

Silence hung in the air, thick with tension. Warren's frustration boiled over, the sudden noise of his palm hitting the table jolted the other patrons, causing them to glance their way. "Then tell me! Why?"

She looked at him, her face etched with the lines of sorrow and grief, "I didn't leave because of you. Ma and Mylan forced me out. Red thought I set you up, and there was a bounty on my head. I came to see you, Warren. So don't act like I didn't."

He chuckled, bitterness in his voice and leaned back in his chair. "Right. A 'visit' about your murder plot. That doesn't qualify."

She exhaled, searching for calm. "The past is the past. What's our next move?"

Warren shifted unease and paused to choose his words. "I'm sorry for what I did and I want to be in Sage's life. I'm going to start therapy. I've stayed clean from drugs. Even got a job. I'm trying to be better."

Nora's eyes widened, surprise laced in her voice. "You didn't deserve to go to prison and I'm sorry for putting you that situation. As much as you like to be in her life that is up to her. Sage has been hurt so much. She barely speaks to me. Why would she want to talk to you?"

His voice cracked in desperation. "What about us then? Are we... are we okay?"

She closed her eyes momentarily. "After everything, after what you did to my girls, we can never be okay." She straightened up, drawing a line. "But there's no animosity. You live your life, I'll live mine. If Sage ever wants to talk, I'll let you know."

"That's... that's good enough for me." Warren's voice was above a whisper as he rose from the chair, his demeanor defeated.

As Warren began to leave, Nora gestured to Donny to come over. "D, do you know someone named Que?"

Donny squinted. "There are many Ques out there. Got any specifics?"

"The one whose stepdad owns the Onyx Sabre Casino," Nora replied, urgency noticeable.

Recognition dawned on Donny. "Oh, that wannabe gangster? Heard he got clipped a few weeks ago. Why?"

Both Warren's and Donny's expressions shifted to concern and surprise. The tension was palpable.

"I need to find out who was behind it," Nora declared, determination in her eyes.

Donny shook his head. "He hung around Beacon Ave. But no one there's gonna spill. Too tight-lipped."

Warren stepped closer, eyes filled with worry. "Nora, what's happening? Do you need help?"

She met his gaze, her tone icy. "You live your life. I live mine." Standing up, she nodded at Donny. "Thanks for the intel, D."

The air was thick with unresolved tensions and lingering questions as Nora strode away.

* * *

Sage, surrounded by the clutter of books and notebooks, stood at her locker. Her attention was focused that she jumped when Cylus's voice broke through her thoughts.

"I haven't seen you much at school," Cylus remarked, a genuine look of concern in his hazel eyes.

Sage hesitated as she met his gaze. "I've been busy," she replied, her fingers fumbling with a textbook.

An awkward silence enveloped them. Cylus shifted from one foot to the other, seeming at a loss for words.

"Is there something you want to say?" Sage prompted, a slight edge to her voice.

Cylus looked down, shook his head in negation, and stepped away. But after a few steps, he stopped, took a deep breath, and spun back around. "Sage, I like you. A lot. And I thought... I thought maybe you felt the same," he admitted.

Sage's gaze remained fixed on the ground, an internal struggle clear in her eyes. Silence stretched between them.

With a sigh of resignation, Cylus murmured, "Maybe I was wrong."

As Sage snapped her locker shut, the metallic clang resonated like a gavel's verdict. She turned to face him. "You weren't wrong," she began, twirling a strand of her hair. "I do like you." Taking a shaky breath, she continued, "But something happened, something personal, and I... I don't think I'm ready for a boyfriend right now."

Cylus's eyes widened in understanding. "Hey, I don't want to push or make you uncomfortable."

"Let me finish," she said, her voice more assertive, taking another steady breath. "I just want you to understand why I've been distant."

He nodded, letting her speak her truth. "I get it, and I respect where you're coming from. But how would you feel about us just... hanging out? No pressure, just as friends?"

A gentle smile illuminated Sage's face, softened her earlier guardedness. "I'd like that," she replied, the tension between them melted away.

As they stood side by side, their conversation veered towards movies. They both laughed upon realizing there was a popular movie neither had seen yet.

"How about we catch it after school?" Cylus suggested, his eyes hopeful.

Sage smiled. "Sounds like a perfect movie date. Just two friends enjoying a film."

Their earlier conversation still weighed on them, but they felt better knowing they had plans to hang out.

As Sage prepared to leave school early, she was stopped by Ms. Collen, the school psychiatrist. The older woman had a firm, concerned expression on her face, her brows furrowed in worry.

"Sage, you're late for class."

"I was just headed there," Sage replied, her voice defensive.

"May I speak with you for a minute?" Ms. Collen inquired as she blocked Sage's path.

Sage hesitated, her posture rigid. Her eyes darted around, not wanting to be held back.

With a deep breath, Ms. Collen began, "I'm just concerned because you haven't been attending our weekly sessions. I've also spoken with your teachers. You're behind in all of your classes. Is everything okay?"

Sage's expression hardened. "I've decided that I no longer need counseling, and my grades in my classes are none of your business."

"As the school psychiatrist, it is my business," Ms. Collen responded with a firm tone, crossing her arms. "You've been skipping class, and some days you don't even attend school. You stopped attending basketball practices. There's obviously something going on."

Huffing, Sage shot back, "First off, I'm not even on the basketball team. I was just the water girl, and I ain't doing that shit anymore. Second, there's nothing going on. You just need to stay in your lane and leave me the hell alone."

Ms. Collen's voice held an edge of warning. "I will call your uncle today. We need to have a meeting."

Sage's face twisted. "If you call my uncle, you're going to regret it."

Ms. Collen's eyes widened, taken aback by the intensity of the threat. "Are you threatening me?" she said.

Taking a bold step towards the older woman, Sage lowered her voice, eyes filled with fire. "That's a promise."

With that, Sage turned on her heel, her footsteps echoing down the hall as she made her way out the front door of the school. The atmosphere in the corridor remained tense, filled with the remnants of the heated confrontation.

Chapter 16

Mended

Sage leaned against the brick wall outside, the day's events weighed heavily on her mind. From a distance, she saw Kamari walking toward her. Even in the busy park, Kamari's vibrant style and confident stride made her stand out.

"You won't believe what Ms. Collen did today," Sage began, her voice dripped with annoyance.

Kamari raised an eyebrow, intrigued. "Oh? What did she do now?"

After a brief rundown of the earlier confrontation with Ms. Collen, Kamari shook her head, chuckling, "Man, that woman seriously needs to chill. Always sticking her nose where it doesn't belong."

Sage nodded in agreement, blowing out a frustrated breath. "Tell me about it."

Kamari shifted, her smirk morphed into a more mischievous grin. "Speaking of drama, guess who I heard about? That girl from the other crew, the one who jumped you."

Sage's interest was immediately piqued. "What about her?"

Kamari leaned in, her voice dropped to a whisper. "There's a kickback tonight in Bedstuy, and word is she's going to be there. How about we pull up on her and give her a little... surprise?"

Sage's lips curled into a matching grin. Her eyes gleamed with anticipation. "So, what's the plan?" she pressed.

"We just set it off when we see her," Kamari said with a shrugged. "Let her feel what it's like to be on the receiving end of her own behavior."

The two shared a moment, their laughter echoed in the cool evening air. Sage held her hand up, and Kamari met it with her own, their palms connected in a triumphant high-five. Whatever the night held for them, they'd face it together.

* * *

Sage and Kamari strolled through the front door of the house, unbothered by the nasty looks that followed them. They had crashed this kickback, a gathering they hadn't received an official invite to, but their confidence remained unshaken. Kamari scanned the room until it landed on one of the girls who helped jump Sage. She pointed her out to Sage. Anger flashed in Sage's eyes. "I'm about to beat her ass."

"Wait, let's play it cool. Remember, this is not our neighborhood," Kamari said.

Sage's gaze pierced through the crowd as she fixated on the girl. "Forget all that. I ain't come here to play it cool. Wasn't you the one talking about setting shit off? Now you're scared."

Kamari faced Sage. "I ain't scared of shit." Kamari pulled out her gun. The sound of the gunshot to the ceiling reverberated through the room, causing a wave of panic and confusion.

Sage's heart pounded in her chest. "What the hell? We said nothing about shooting. What's wrong with you?"

People scrambled to escape the house. Kamari signaled for Sage to go after the girl. Before she could run out, Sage caught a grip of her braids, pulling her to the ground and pounded her face. The fight went on for a while before blue and red lights flashed, casting an eerie glow over the house.

As handcuffs closed around Sage's wrists, the weight of her choices became evident. Her heart pounded in her chest, her mind raced with a mixture of fear and uncertainty. She had never been arrested before. Her palms grew clammy, and a knot formed in the pit of her stomach.

* * *

Nora burst through the doors of the police station. Her eyes locked onto a uniformed officer behind the front desk, and she wasted no time in making her presence known. "I am looking for Sage Woods."

The officer stood from her desk and headed towards the back of the station. The officer later returned with detective Douglas. "Hello, Miss Woods. Nice to see you again. Detective Douglas escorted her to an interrogation room, where Sage was seated. Nora entered the room and took a seat next to Sage.

"I told you to call my uncle. What is she doing here?" Sage uttered.

"Shut your mouth," Nora said. "What is going on? Why is Sage being questioned?" Nora directed her questions to detective Douglas.

Douglas took a seat across from them. "Tonight, Sage and her friend Kamari went to someone's home. A gun was fired, and a girl was badly beaten."

Sage's heart sank as she felt the weight of Nora's gaze bearing down on her. The surrounding air grew heavy with tension as a silence settled between them. Nora returned her attention to detective Douglas. "Whose gun was it?"

"It was Kamari's, however, Sage assaulted a girl. She is currently in the hospital recovering."

Douglas was interrupted by his partner, detective Matthew. "Hello ladies, Sage, I just had a question for you. The girl that you attacked tonight reported that she took part in the attack that happened to you a month ago. From my recollection, you stated you did not know who the girls were that assaulted you."

Nora's hand gently rested on Sage's lap, halting Sage from uttering a response. "Is my daughter being charged with something?"

"No, the girl does not want to press charges, however, she reported her friend has been missing for over a week now." Matthew intertwined his fingers and leaned forward. "Do you know anything about that?"

"I don't like your line of questioning, detective. Now, if my daughter is not being charged with anything, then she has nothing else to say."

Nora and Sage rose from their seats and headed towards the door.

"If we have any more questions, we know where to find you," detective Douglas added.

Nora and Sage walked through the bustling corridors of the police station, their footsteps echoed against the sterile walls. As they made their way, Sage's gaze at a nearby cell where Kamari was being held. Nora noticed the silent exchange between Sage and Kamari. She glanced at Kamari with narrowed eyes.

***

Nora, Mylan, and Sarah sat around the table. The room felt heavy with unspoken words; the silence heightened by the weight of their emotions. Nora's brows furrowed, her eyes fixed sternly on Sage, her lips pressed into a thin line.

"What y'all want me to say?" Sage said.

Nora slammed her fists onto the table with a resounding thud. "The truth. What the hell happened at the party? Who is this Kamari girl you've been hanging out with? Have you lost your mind?"

Sage, surprised by the force of Nora's outburst. "Now you want to act like you care."

"Don't you dare flip this shit on me. What did you do?"

Mylan chimed in, "We can't help you if you don't tell us what happened."

Sage's eyes darted around the room, unable to settle on any-one point of focus. Her palms grew sweaty as she wiped them onto her pants. "I knew who jumped me that day. I didn't want to say anything because I thought I could handle it on my own."

"Why didn't you tell us?" Mylan asked.

"Y'all can't fight my battles for me. I'm a big girl."

Mylan's eyes narrowed. "Who's this Kamari chick you've been hanging out with?"

"Just some girl from around the way. She looks out for me and I look out for her. She's my best friend."

"Bullshit. I saw that woman. She is way too old to be your best friend. She looks like she could be in her twenties," Nora said.

A lump formed in Sage's throat, a thickness that made it difficult to speak. She swallowed hard, trying to ease the tightness that strangled her vocal cords.

"I don't want you hanging around that girl anymore," Nora demanded.

Sage banged an open palm on the table. "You can't make me stop hanging out with her. Let's be for real."

"I'm going to show you how for real I am. I will pick you up from school starting tomorrow. You can hate me all you want. I will not let you mess up your life."

"Oh, you mean like you did." Sage raised from her seat. "Well guess what Mercy. I am my mother's daughter."

Sage bolted towards her room, her feet carrying her with a sense of urgency. Each step echoed with a resounding thud. Sarah hurriedly followed Sage, her hand instinctively cradling her pregnant stomach.

Mylan poured a bottle of Moscato into two wine glasses and he held one glass out to Nora, a silent offering of solace and distraction from their troubles. Nora's eyes, tired and burdened, met Mylan's gaze as she accepted the glass. She took a big gulp, finishing the drink in seconds. "I left my daughters with you because I thought you would take care of them."

"Excuse me," Mylan gently set his wineglass down on the sleek kitchen island. "I have been taking care of your children for almost a year. You got some damn nerve."

"Sage wouldn't be in the situation if you were," Nora hissed.

"I had a driver for both of them after Sage got jumped, but neither of them wanted it. I can't watch Sage's every movement. She is going to hang out with whoever she wants to. Everyday Avery comes into this house and storms off to her room and locks the door until the next morning. I am not a goddamn therapist."

Nora's eyes narrowed. "I'm not asking you to be. I just need your eyes on them more."

Mylan walked around the island and stood inches away from Nora. "I am not their father either, Nora."

Nora crossed her arms. "I know you're not their father, Mylan." But you are a part of their lives. They need a positive role model, someone who can guide them and be there for them when I can't."

Mylan shook his head. "I sell illegal guns for a living. I don't know how much of a positive role model I can be. It seems like you want me to be their parent instead of you."

She took a step back, processing his words. "That is not true."

"Tell me, what is true, Nora?"

Deep down, Nora carried a nagging worry that her actions would drive her daughters away, just as her own mother had pushed her away in the past. Fear and guilt whispered in her mind, Nora struggled to admit her vulnerabilities. "I'm scared that I will push them away the way mom did me," she finally confessed.

"I'm no different from her. Shit, I'm probably worst. What kind of parent am I? Henry is dead because of me. Because of my selfishness." Nora's voice caught in her throat, her attempt to speak stifled by a sudden surge of emotion. "Because of my greed. I am a terrible person... a terrible mother."

Mylan wrapped his arm around Nora's shoulder. "You're not a terrible person. You made terrible mistakes. I know you're trying to do better for yourself, but don't forget that you have to make it right with your girls. They have me and Sarah, but what they need is a mother. It won't be easy, but you just have to try."

Nora embraced him with a heartfelt hug. Her arms wrapped around him, pulling him close as if seeking solace and a sense of security within their sibling bond.

Chapter 17

Alliances

Sarah tapped softly on the door to Sage's room before nuzzling it open. "May I come in?"

"You don't need my permission. This is your house," Sage hissed.

Sarah positioned herself close to Sage on her bed. "Are you okay?

Tears welled up in Sage's eyes. "I wish I had died that night when they killed my dad. It would have been so much easier than this." Slowly, she slid off the edge of the bed and crumbled onto the floor. With her knees drawn close to her chest. "I'm not okay. Even though I know he is in prison and never getting out. It keeps replaying in my head." Sage hit her head repeatedly. "It won't go away."

Sarah cradled her wrist to stop her from hurting herself. "I cannot possibly know what you're feeling. Healing is possible, but forgetting is not."

Sage glanced at Sarah. "How do you know?"

With a subtle gesture, she motioned for Sage to rise, her hand reaching out to intertwine their fingers. "The first step to healing is acknowledging what hurt you. Tell me what hurt you."

Sage's head bowed low. A veil of shame fell upon her. Sarah asked her again. Sage's gaze met Sarah's as her head rose. "I was... raped."

"How does that make you feel?"

A single tear fell to Sage's cheek. "I feel disgusted with myself and angry."

Sarah's voice, firm and gentle, "Repeat after me," she instructed, her tone filled with support.

Sage hesitated for a moment, then nodded, ready to shed the weight of her shame. Taking a deep breath, she mirrored Sarah's words. "No weapon formed against me shall prosper and every tongue that rises against me in judgment shall be condemned."

"You have now taken back your control," Sarah assured her.

Sage embraced with a warm hug. "Thank you."

As Sarah departed from Sage's room, Sage's hand reached into her pocket, retrieving a small bag of cocaine and threw it into the trash.

* * *

Tegan withdrew a textbook from her locker, engrossed in a conversation with Cylus. As they exchanged words, Sage cautiously approached them, her apprehension gnawing at her. Doubts crept in, whispering that perhaps they had no interest in speaking to her. "Hey y'all, Wassup," she said nervously.

Cylus and Tegan exchanged looks. Tegan broke the silence, her voice filled with warmth. "Hey," she said, a smile playing at the corners of her lips. "It's been a minute."

Cylus looked down at his phone as he remained silent. Tegan's cheerfulness wavered as she caught onto Cylus's silence, sensing the tension in the air. "We were just talking about the cheerleaders' competition that's happening later today. You should come? I mean, that's if you are not busy."

"You know she's too cool for school events or friends or boyfriends," Cylus chimed in.

Tegan's eyebrows raised, surprised by Cylus' comment. She paused for a moment, processing his words, unsure if it was a playful jab or a genuine observation. A half-smile formed on her lips. "Um-

Sage's reply came quickly, her eyes fixed on Cylus. "I'd love to join. It sounds like a good time," she said, her words brimmed with enthusiasm.

"That's great. I'll save you a seat," Tegan responded, her voice carried a note of relief. After sensing the tension in the air, she bowed out gracefully. "Now, I'm going to leave because this tension is making me uncomfortable," she added. Tegan turned to leave, to allow Sage and Cylus the space they needed to talk.

"Yeah, I'm about to head out too," he said as he turned to leave.

Sage gently grabbed his forearm. "Wait, can we talk?"

"Ain't shit for us to talk about. You clearly ain't messing with me. I'm not about to chase you."

"It's not even like that," Sage said.

"So what is it like then?" he questioned. "I asked you on a date and you stood me up! I also don't want to hear no bullshit about your uncle not letting you go out because I know that's cap," he declared, not willing to entertain any evasive explanations.

"You're right," she admitted, her voice filled with a hint of regret. "I got caught up with the wrong people and I was only thinking about myself. That's on me, but that doesn't change how I feel about you."

"But it changes how I feel about you." He took a moment to gather his thoughts, his gaze still fixed on Sage's face. "I don't hate you, Sage," he continued, his voice gentle. "I just feel like we are better off as friends." Cylus took a small step back, creating a bit of distance between them.

Cylus patted her shoulder with a smile and walked away. There was a touch of sadness in Sage's eyes as she watched him leave. Sage glanced down at her vibrating cell phone, her eyes fixated on the caller ID that displayed Kamari's name. A mix of emotions swirled within her, but with a heavy sigh, she declined the call.

Tegan and Sage walked out of school, laughter bubbling between them as they discussed the competition winners. Sage's gaze shifted towards Cylus, her eyes briefly catching his figure as he walked past, accompanied by the basketball team and a group of girls. Tegan's eyes followed Sage's gaze, noticing her attention drawn towards Cylus as he passed by, "How did that conversation go?" Tegan asked.

Sage responded, her voice casual as she shrugged her shoulders. "We're just friends," she explained, emphasizing her lack of concern. "I've got to prioritize getting my grades up, anyway."

"That's funny. You haven't been prioritizing me."

Sage's eyes widened as she recognized the voice coming from behind her. She slowly turned around, her heart sinking as she faced Kamari.

"That's because she is not interested in speaking to you," Tegan said with narrowed eyes.

Tegan received a scornful glare from Kamari. "Was I speaking to you?"

Tegan approached Kamari, closing the distance until they were standing inches apart. The air crackled with tension as they locked eyes, neither one willing to back down.

Sage positioned herself between Tegan and Kamari. With a serious look on her face, she met Tegan's gaze. "Yo, hold up," Sage said, her voice laced with a hint of attitude. "I need a minute alone with Kamari. This is between us, so step back for now."

Tegan let out an exaggerated eye roll as she scoffed at Kamari. Dismissing her with a wave of her hand, she turned on her heels and walked away.

Kamari focused her attention on Sage. "Where the hell have you been? I've been calling and texting you."

Sage's gaze darted around her attempt to avoid eye contact with Kamari. "My mom told me I couldn't hang out with you anymore."

"The same mother that killed your father," Kamari said.

"Keep your voice down," Sage hissed. "I'm just trying to get my shit together, stay low, and then we can hang out again once she is off my back."

"Don't you see what she is trying to do? She wants to separate us. You're like my little sister. I love you. She doesn't love you how I do?" Kamari stated.

Sage sighed, "As much as I despise her right now. She's still my mother."

Kamari held on to Sage's hand. "If she loved you, then why aren't you still living in Buffalo? Why is your father dead? And let's not forget, you were raped. None of this would have happened if it weren't for her actions." Kamari stated, her words cutting through the air with a painful truth.

Sage felt Kamari's words hit her like a punch to the gut, the weight of reality crashing down on her with full force. It was like a heavy blow that left her gasping for air. Sage fell into an uneasy silence.

"Your mother, she ain't tryna see us be friends," Kamari's voice cut through the air, laced with frustration. "She knows if you get close to me, you might just find the strength to confront her, to make her pay for what she did to you. That's why she can't be trusted, Sage," Kamari uttered.

"What are you saying?" Sage asked.

"Your mother has to be added to the chopping block?"

Sage's eyes widened with disbelief as she stared at Kamari. "You really expect me to take it to that level? To kill my mother?"

"No mercy can be shown for what she did," Kamari declared. She was firm in her belief that Nora deserved no leniency for the pain she had inflicted on Sage. "The same goes for the rest of the girls that jumped you. We still have two more and one in the hospital. We can't let them get away with hurting you."

The loud honk of a car startled Sage, pulling her back from her deep thoughts. She looked toward the noise and saw Nora getting out of her car. Nora hurriedly made her way towards the girls. "Sage, get in the car," she demanded, her voice leaving no room for argument. Sage pursued her command.

"You better stay away from my child," she demanded, her tone sharp and laced with a warning.

A sly smile crept onto Kamari's face as she responded, "That's up to Sage to decide, and I don't think she's ready to cut ties with me." Kamari sniffed around, "Is that jealousy I smell?"

Nora's voice dropped to a low, dangerous whisper. "If you ever dare come near my daughter again, I won't hesitate to end you. Don't test me, little girl."

Nora strutted back to her car and peeled off, leaving Kamari in her wake. Kamari stood there, her face twisted with a fierce glare.

Chapter 18

Pain

Nora was slammed into a seat, her body jolted with the force. She found herself face-to-face with Harry, their eyes locked in a fierce with an unyielded stare. His steady hand grazed his chin with an air of dominance. The message was crystal clear. He held the power in that moment.

"When I assign someone a task, they tend to get it done," Harry remarked, his words laced with a hint of authority.

Nora's words lingered on the tip of her tongue, but before she could utter a sound, Harry swiftly raised his hand, silencing her with a commanding gesture. "I don't want to hear shit you have to say." Harry stood and sat on the edge of his desk. He gestured to his bodyguards.

Nora's arms were yanked back and tightly bound behind the chair, leaving her immobilized. The chilling presence of a blade against her neck sent shivers down her spine. To reason with Harry, she pleaded, her voice tinged with urgency. "Wait, hold up! I swear, I promised I'd handle the job. I've just been dealing with some family shit," Nora desperately pleaded.

Harry, with his Italian charm, rose and pulled out a brown envelope. "Wanna know why I chose you?" he asked, holding Nora's gaze.

Nora remained silent, her lips tightly sealed as she awaited Harry's next move.

"Because I knew the infamous Nora Mercy Woods would get the job done. You think I need you monitoring my casino grounds?" Harry chuckled, his voice dripped with confidence. "I need you out there, making moves for me and my empire on the streets."

He spread his arms wide, emphasizing his point. "Your first task was to track down the person who took my stepson's life. And what did you do? Couldn't even deliver on that. Don't tell me all those stories about you are nothing but hot air."

"I told you I would get it done. I just have some family issues. I'm telling you the truth," Nora responded.

"Blah, blah, blah. You think I give a damn about your family? As a matter of fact," Harry sneered, as he pulled out a stack of photos from the brown envelope and thrust them in front of Nora's face.

Her eyes widened in shock as she stared at the photos, her heart pounded in her chest. "What the fuck is this?" she exclaimed.

"I thought, why just go after your daughters when I can take your whole damn family out, including your brother, his wife, and your baby's daddy?" Harry sneered, a wicked grin spread across his face. "All in the family."

"What the hell is your problem? She screamed. In a split second, her eyes darted to the knife pressed against her neck.

"When I give you a task, I expect it to be fucking done," Harry asserted, his voice laced with a gritty edge. His pierced gaze locked onto Nora and left no room for negotiation. "I've got eyes everywhere, so don't even think about snitching to the police."

Nora was forcefully let go from the chair and thrown out of the office, and crashed onto the floor. The door slammed shut behind her, leaving her defeated and with a bitter taste in her mouth.

* * *

Sage sat in the passenger seat, while Avery occupied the back, immersed in her own world with her Sony headphones on. Nora drove in silence, the car filled with a quiet stillness.

Sage realized they were headed in a different direction than Mylan's condo. Curiosity tugged at her, and she couldn't help but ask, "Where are we going?"

Nora stayed silent until they arrived at a gravesite. "We're here to visit your grandma," Nora replied. She stepped out of the car, and Sage followed suit and got out onto the ground.

However, Avery stayed inside, refusing to move. Nora gently tapped on the window as she urged Avery to exit the car.

"I don't want to go," Avery protested from behind the closed window.

Nora's voice grew louder. "I'm not asking you. Now, let's go!"

"Leave me alone!" Avery screamed as she swiftly put her headphones back in her ears.

Nora glanced up at Sage, frustration clear on her face. "What the hell is her problem?" she questioned.

Sage rolled her eyes in response. "Let's just go. I'm over it," she replied.

Nora and Sage walked on the well-kept grass towards Laverne's tombstone.

Nora tucked her hands into her pockets, her eyes fixed on the words etched into Laverne's tombstone. "A mother, a sister, and a friend," she whispered, her voice tinged with sorrow.

Sage chuckled. The sound carried a hint of irony. Nora glanced at her, curiosity etched on her face as she wondered what had sparked the amusement.

"You really thought we were going to come here and have some kind of Cumbaya moment," Sage remarked.

"I was only bringing you here because I thought that-

"You thought what? That I would cry and run into your arms? You ruined my life, Nora. I'll never forgive you," Sage declared, as she cut her off.

As Sage's words hung in the air, Nora turned away, her emotions welled up. The brim of her eyelids threatened to overflow, tears pooled just beneath the surface. "Laverne treated me like I was the ugly bigfoot stepchild," Nora admitted, her voice heavy with hurt.

"I guess the apple doesn't fall too far from the tree," Sage responded.

She beckoned for Sage to listen. Her voice carried a weight of unfinished thoughts. "As a child, I never knew why she hated me so much," Nora admitted. "The irony of it all is she only paid attention to me when I was doing something wrong. So, that's what I did."

Sage listened intently, her eyes fixed on Nora's face.

"I got into fights at school, failed my classes, robbed, cheated, and," Nora's voice trailed off as she locked eyes with Sage, "Killed."

Sage's face remained unaffected by Nora's admission of taking someone's life. She had already known about the darkness within her mother, so this revelation didn't come as a surprise. "Why are you telling me this?"

"The point I'm tryna make is, I did all that shit because I thought it was the only way Laverne would show me some love. I craved her attention, but I got caught up in the street life. I let it consume me, mess with my head. I started hurting the ones who mattered most, and I don't want you going down that same path."

"All that proves is our childhoods were messed up in their own ways," Sage sighed. "The only difference is you made choices that led you down that path. I wanted none of this. You schemed and plotted without considering the consequences." Sage's eyes welled up with tears. "They took away my innocence. You can't possibly understand what that feels like."

"Baby, I'm sor- Nora's voice trailed off as Sage turned away, tears streamed down her cheeks.

Nora reached out for a hug, but Sage hesitated, unsure whether to accept the gesture. As Sage's tears continued to flow, the longing for a comforting embrace grew stronger. Finally, they embraced, finding solace in each other's arms. "I love you," Nora whispered.

Once the tears had ceased, they linked their arms together and made their way back to the car. As they walked, Nora caught sight of something on Sage's inner wrist. "Is that a tattoo?" she asked.

Sage nodded apprehensively as she feared Nora's reaction. Nora inquired about the tattoo, and Sage mustered the courage to reply, "It says 'Sweetie'."

Nora's smile widened as she reminisced, "Henry used to call you that when you were just a little one. Can't believe that you remember. I actually like it."

Chapter 19

Shattered

"Ayo, Sage. What's up?" Donny yelled as he leaned up against his car.

As Sage walked out of school, her eyes caught sight of Donny, leaning nonchalantly against his sleek BMW. She couldn't help but feel a flicker of excitement at the sight of him. "Donny, what are you doing here?"

"Damn, I need permission to see my baby cousin," he said.

Sage approached Donny with Tegan by her side, introducing them to each other. She reminded Donny of their previous encounter at the street basketball game, hoping to spark his memory.

Tegan greeted Donny with a flirtatious smile and a playful "Hi handsome," her eyes sparkling with mischief.

Sage nudged her arm. "Anyway, what are you doing here?"

"I haven't seen you since the game. I just wanted to check in with you."

As Donny checked in with her, Sage felt a sense of appreciation for his concern. However, it also reminded her of Warren, and the painful memory of him that lingered in the back of her mind. "I know the last conversation we had wasn't great," Sage admitted.

Donny wrapped his arm around her neck. "It's all good. I ain't mad at cha."

A sense of relief washed over Sage, and a smile crept onto her face. In that moment, she felt a weight lifted off her shoulders, knowing that she had someone like Donny who cared about her well-being.

"It's Friday. I was thinking we hit up Coney Island. Play a few games and get on some rides. What y'all think?" Donny looked at Sage and Tegan as he awaited their response.

"What's Coney Island?" Sage asked.

Donny and Tegan exchanged glances. They busted into laughter, unable to contain their disbelief. "It's an amusement park," Tegan replied as she chuckled.

"I'm always down for some fun," Sage laughed as she joined in on the laughter.

Donny called out to Cylus and invited him to join them at Coney Island. Cylus glanced at Sage and then back at Donny as he considered the invitation. After a moment of thought, he tagged along. They all piled into Donny's car, eager for the adventure ahead. Sage quickly sent a text to Nora to inform her of their plans.

***

Donny's presence did not go unnoticed as they entered the bustling amusement park. He was greeted by familiar faces at every turn, leaving little room for him to catch his breath.

Donny and Cylus walked ahead, leaving Sage and Tegan slightly behind. Tegan broke the silence. "Are you two gonna say anything? This silence between you y'all is hella awkward." Tegan locked her arm with Sages. "It is so obvious that he likes you."

"We're just friends, remember," Sage reminded.

Tegan let out an exasperated sigh and rolled her eyes. "He only said that because he thinks you're not interested," she retorted. Determined to take matters into her own hands, she pulled Cylus back slightly and whispered into his ear and suggested that Sage wanted to play the basketball shootout game with him. Tegan walked off with Donny, leaving the two alone.

"Let's do it," Cylus replied with a smile, ready for the challenge.

Sage returned the smile and set the rules. "First one to 25 points wins," she declared, as she got into position for the basketball shootout game.

"Don't forget, I am the captain of the basketball team," Cylus joked.

"Don't worry, I won't go easy on you," Sage teased back, as they bumped shoulders. They both positioned themselves at the basketball hoop, ready to showcase their skills. The friendly competition began as each of them aimed to reach that winning score of 25 points.

Sage and Cylus laughed and played as they tossed the ball and blocked each other's shots. Their joy and competitiveness filled the air, adding to the lively atmosphere. Sage scored the last shot, narrowly beating Cylus by just one point. The thrill of victory lit up her face as she celebrated her win. As excitement bubbled inside her, Sage jumped into Cylus' arms. He held her gently, his hands softly caressed her back as they shared the joy of the moment.

Sage gently pulled back from Cylus's embrace and looked up into his warm brown eyes. She felt something stir within her, a spark of electricity that made her heart race and her senses heightened. Sage swallowed hard and took a step back. A hint of a smile played on her lips. "I guess I've got some skills," she said, her voice filled with playful pride.

Cylus slipped his hands into his pockets, a charming smile tugged at the corners of his lips. "Yeah, something like that," he replied, his tone light and playful.

Sage and Cylus stood in a momentary silence, their gazes locked and an unspoken tension hung in the air.

Tegan rushed over, "Yo, we about to get on the Cyclone."

After she learned the Cyclone was a roller coaster, Sage's anxiety kicked in. Her fear of heights made her nervous about the idea of getting on the ride. Sage glanced up at the towering ride, and a knot formed in her stomach.

Cylus leaned in close and whispered in her ear, "I got you." He gripped her hand as they made their way towards the seats. Once they were strapped in, Sage squeezed Cylus's hand tighter. "It's not as bad as you think."

"Says the person who is not afraid of heights. I feel like my stomach is about to fall out of my ass." They both laughed.

As the ride took off, Sage felt an exhilarated rush course through her veins. As the ride whirled around, twisting and turning, Cylus clenched her hand, never letting go. Sage let out a joyful "woo!" as the excitement of the ride took her over.

As they strolled through the amusement park, Sage and Cylus remained oblivious to the fact that they were still holding hands. Cylus paused and looked at Sage, a tender expression on his face. "You finally faced your fears. How does it feel?" he asked, his voice filled with admiration.

"It feels amazing," Sage replied, a wide smile spread across her face. "I can't remember the last time I had this much fun. It seems like ever since I got here, it's been nothing but drama.

So, it's a relief to feel like a regular teenager, enjoying myself. And I'm glad I got to do it with you," she added.

Cylus's hand caressed Sage's chin as he leaned in for a kiss, but before their lips could meet, they were interrupted by Donny's voice. "Hold up, Cylus. You know you're my boy, but this is still my cousin. Keep your lips to yourself," Donny interjected.

Tegan stood there with a playful smile as she observed the interaction between Sage, Cylus, and Donny. Her eyes twinkled with amusement as she enjoyed the moment.

Amid their joyful moment, chaos erupted as a fight broke out in the park. Donny urged Sage and Tegan to go to the car, but Cylus hesitated, unwilling to leave Donny alone in the midst of the turmoil. As Sage and Tegan made their way to the car, their hearts pounded with fear. Multiple shots rang out, sending shockwaves through the air.

Sage's footsteps slowed as she cautiously approached the direction of the gunfire. Her worry about Cylus and Donny consumed her thoughts. Tegan tried to stop her, but Sage continued walking. With each step, her heart pounded in her chest. As she reached the front of the amusement park, her worst fears were realized, which caused her heart to drop in sheer terror.

Donny was hunched over Cylus's body, blood stained the ground beneath them. Sage's legs gave way beneath her as she rushed to the ground. A piercing scream escaped her lips. Tegan took out her phone. Her hands trembled as she dialed for an ambulance, desperately seeking help.

Chapter 20

Betrayal

Donny paced restlessly back and forth in the hospital waiting area, his anxiety palpable. Meanwhile, Sage sat hunched over, her body shaking with uncontrollable sobs. Tegan, her face etched with concern, sat beside Sage, offering gentle words of comfort.

Nora and Mylan entered the hospital with furrowed brows and restless eyes, their worry etched deeply into their faces. Their steps were quick, driven by a sense of urgency and concern. As Nora and Mylan approached Sage, their eyes couldn't help but notice Donny, still pacing back and forth. "What happened?" Nora asked.

Before Sage spoke, Paulette and Warren's entrance silenced the room. Time stood still as Warren and Sage locked eyes with tension and pain. Sage's heart skipped a beat as memories flooded her mind, reminding her of the last time she had laid eyes on her father. "What is he doing here?" Sage blurted out.

Warren leaned towards Paulette, his voice barely above a whisper, "I think it's best if I go."

Sage stood up, her voice filled with determination. "Nah, don't leave now. Don't be a coward."

Mylan reached out and tried to hold her back, as he whispered, "Not here, not now." But Sage shrugged off his grip and stood her ground.

Sage's voice trembled with anger as she confronted her father, "You come up here acting all concerned. Did you come for Donny or for me? Mr. 'devoted' father. How about you tell everyone in this damn hospital how you let someone rape me?"

"Sage, let's not do this here," Nora interjected, her voice filled with concern.

Warren's eyes darted around the room, his silence spoke volumes. The weight of Sage's words hung heavily in the air, leaving him at a loss for words.

Sage's voice pierced through the tense atmosphere. Her anger and pain echoed in her words. She confronted Warren directly and demanded the truth to be exposed. The room fell silent. Everyone held their breath, awaiting Warren's response.

Warren's voice trembled with remorse. "I'm sorry."

Sage's eyes welled up with tears as she uttered, "I'm sorry. Is that all?" Her gaze shifted between Nora and Warren. "You two are made for each other, aren't you? Thinking that a simple 'I'm sorry' can fix everything. Y'all make me sick."

"I am still your mother," Nora muttered.

"Neither one of you knows what it means to be a parent." She walked over to Tegan and sat beside her. Tegan placed a comforting hand on Sage's back, offering silent support.

Warren cleared his throat, his voice filled with regret. "I know I messed up. I don't have anyone to blame but myself," he began. "The person you met was not who I am. I was lost and broken, and I let my own demons cloud my judgment. I know a simple sorry will not make you forgive me, but I want you to know that I care about you. Whether you want to hear it, I do." With those words, Warren turned and walked out of the waiting area, leaving behind a heavy silence.

Sage's eyes welled up with tears, shimmered with unspoken sadness. Her brows furrowed, mirroring the heaviness in her heart.

Moments later, the doctor entered the waiting area, his face devoid of any discernible emotion. Clutching a folder in his hands, he scanned the room and asked, "Are you the family of Cylus Wesley?" His voice remained calm and composed, giving away nothing of the news he held within the confines of that folder.

Donny's hands trembled slightly as he clutched onto the edge of the chair, his eyes darting back and forth between the doctor and the folder. His face was etched with concern, his brows furrowed and his lips pressed together in a tight line. "I'm his friend," Donny replied. "I was with him when he was shot. Is he okay?"

"I understand your concern, but I'm unable to share any information with you at the moment. We need to speak with his parents first, as they are the authorized guardians. Once they have been updated, they can provide you with the information." The doctor's voice remained professional, yet empathetic, as he acknowledged Donny's eagerness for updates.

Sage stood by Donny's side, her voice tinged with worry. "What do we do now?"

Donny placed a comforting hand on Sage's shoulder, his voice filled with reassurance. "Don't worry, Sage. Cylus's parents are flying in from San Francisco. They'll be here soon."

Donny made a firm promise to Sage as they prepared to leave the hospital. "I promise, Sage. I will find out who did this to Cylus. They won't get away with it."

Outside the hospital, Sage and Tegan trailed behind Nora and Mylan, heading towards the car. Just as they were about to reach their destination, Paulette hurriedly approached Sage. Sage instructed Tegan to go ahead to the car.

"You don't know me, but I'm your-

Sage interrupted, "I know who you are. I just don't know why you want to talk to me."

"I understand that you have a lot going on, and I don't want to add to your burden," Paulette spoke gently. "Perhaps now isn't the best time. I just wanted to meet my granddaughter." Paulette reached out and handed Sage a piece of paper with her phone number written on it. "Take your time, and when you're ready, call me."

Sage took a deep breath as she turned and made her way towards the car.

Kamari laughed and joked with her friends in the park, playing a dice game. They gathered closely, enjoying the fun and friendly atmosphere. Kamari's laughter subsided, and she stopped mid-game as her friend nudged her and showed someone approaching. Kamari turned around, her eyes narrowing as she locked her gaze with Sage's. "I'm surprised your mother let you out of the house."

Sage's shoulders were slightly slumped, and her eyes seemed lost in the distance. As Kamari glanced at Sage, a flicker of concern flashed across her face. She could sense that something was wrong. "I heard about your man. He good?"

"He's awake now, but won't complete the school year. That's not why I'm here."

"What's up? What you need? You know I always got you," Kamari replied.

Sage rubbed the back of her neck. "I need a rock," she murmured.

Kamari quickly glanced around to ensure that their conversation remained private. A knowing look passed between her and Sage, as she understood Sage was requesting cocaine, which they had indulged in together before. "I don't think right now is the time for that."

Sage exhaled heavily. "Just hook me up."

Kamari discreetly handed Sage a small bag, making it seem like a casual exchange of a high-five. Sage slid the bag into her pocket. "You ready to finish these other girls?"

Kamari's smile widened, a mischievous glint in her eyes. "That's already been taken care of. All you gotta do is handle the one in the hospital. I heard she's getting out tomorrow." Kamari placed her arm over her shoulder. "I was thinking we would bust into her room and smother her with a pillow." Kamari laughed.

"I was thinking something faster. You got a piece on you?" Sage asked.

Kamari discreetly passed her a weapon, which she tucked into her waistband. "This time will be a breeze. You've already done it twice before. This is nothing," Kamari reassured. "I'll be right there with you."

Sage smirked and tapped the pocket that held the cocaine. "Let's go hit this."

Kamari chuckled, her arm still draped around Sage's shoulders, as they walked away together.

Chapter 21

Consequences

Beacon Ave was bustling with activity as people gathered on street corners, smoking and chatting. Nora surveyed her surroundings, taking in the vibrant urban atmosphere that surrounded her. Nora moved through the bustling crowd, discreetly seeking information about Que's whereabouts.

She approached various individuals, but their lips remained sealed, refusing to divulge any information. As she continued her search, she couldn't help but notice two men in the distance engaged in hushed conversation while keeping a close eye on her.

Nora cautiously approached the two men, keeping her guard up. "What's up?" she asked, trying to strike up a conversation.

The men exchanged glances, their expressions guarded as they crossed their arms, creating an air of skepticism.

"Y'all know somebody named Que?"

One man ran a hand across his face. "Nah, never heard of that name before," he replied, his tone nonchalant.

"Listen, I know he got killed out here recently. Y'all know anything about that?" Nora inquired.

They both laughed and turned to walk away, dismissing Nora's question as they walked off. Nora swiftly ran in front of them, raising her phone to capture their picture. "What the hell you doing, lady?" another man yelled in protest.

"I'll be sending this picture to Harry Sagen and letting him know that you two killed Que," Nora declared firmly before turning away.

One man scratched his head, a look of uncertainty on his face. "Hold up, don't go doing that. You ain't no cop, right?" He quickly glanced around, checking for any unwanted attention. "We don't want no trouble, you know?"

Nora smirked, "Nah, I ain't no cop. But I know people who can make your lives a living hell if they find out the truth. So, you better start talking before shit gets real messy."

"Listen, I ain't tryna get killed by Chuckie. She already had one of her men pull up on us. I ain't fucking around with her. That girl is psycho."

"Who the fuck is this Chuckie person? Is that who killed Que?"

Both men hesitated, giving each other suspicious looks. Their expressions showed they were unsure whether to reveal the truth. "It wasn't Chuckie. She sent someone else to kill Que? Some young girl."

Nora asked who the girl was, eager to find out her name.

Nora's ears rang as a bullet whizzed past her, striking both men. She instinctively dropped to the ground, trying to evade the flying bullets. Her gaze flickered up towards the unmarked black car, but its occupant remained hidden. Crawling towards one of the injured men, she pleaded with him to reveal a name. Blood gushed from his chest as she frantically covered the wound with her hands. "Tell me a name, give me a name," she demanded, her voice trembling with urgency.

As he slipped into unconsciousness, blood dripped from his mouth. He weakly whispered, "Sweetie."

Moments later, Nora sat in her car, bloodstained and disoriented. Her head spun as the man's voice echoed in her mind, repeating the name, "Sweetie." She couldn't deny the thoughts racing through her mind. An image of Sage's "sweetie" tattoo flashed vividly, intensifying her unease. Nora swiftly grabbed her phone and dialed a number, her voice filled with urgency as she issued the command, "Meet me at the spot."

Nora arrived at the mall parking lot and parked her car. Mylan, Sarah, Donny, and Warren were already there, anxiously waiting. Nora stepped out of the car, her body still stained with blood. Mylan rushed to Nora's side, concern etched on his face. "What the hell happened?" He gently patted her body, checking for any signs of injury.

"It's not my blood. I'm fine," she assured him.

Sarah stroked her pregnant stomach, her brows furrowed with concern. "Why did you bring us here? Is something wrong? Are we in trouble?" she asked, her voice laced with worry.

Donny looked at Nora, his hands fidgeting. "What's up?" he asked

Mylan leaned closer to Nora, his voice low. "What are they doing here?" he whispered, nodding towards Warren and Donny.

Nora positioned herself in front of them, her tone serious. "We have a problem?" she sighed. "A big one."

They exchanged glances. Their eyes shifted between each other and then back to Nora, anticipating her explanation.

Nora explained the task that Harry had assigned her.

"I don't understand what any of this has to do with us," Warren said, his voice filled with confusion. "Did you find out who did it?"

Nora took a deep breath and explained, "I found these guys on Beacon. They said someone named Chuckie sent one of her people to kill Que. The person goes by the name Sweetie."

"Who is this sweetie person?" Sarah question.

Donny glanced at Nora, his eyes widening with realization. "Shit. It's Sage, isn't it?" He clenched his fist and struck his palm in frustration. "I knew something like this would happen."

"Who the fuck is Chuckie?" Mylan asked.

"Kamari!" Donny uttered.

"The bitch she got arrested with the other night," Mylan said.

Warren's eyes widened in shock as he turned to Nora. "She was arrested?" His voice trembled with concern. "Why didn't you tell me?"

"Wait, you knew she was hanging out with this Chuckie, Kamari person and ain't say shit!" Nora yelled.

Sarah's voice cut through the heated argument, silencing everyone for a moment. She stood there, her hand rested on her belly, her eyes were heavy. "Nora, I know we haven't known each other for long, but every time you're around, chaos follows. Right now, Mylan and I have our own lives to think about, our own future to protect. We can't be a part of this. Please, leave us out of it." Sarah looked at Mylan, silently urging him to support her decision.

Mylan nodded wearily, his voice tinged with exhaustion. "She's got a point. It's always drama when you're around, and I have to prioritize the safety of my family. This time, I can't be involved."

Nora's voice cracked as she screamed, "I am your family!"

"Are you really considering going up against Harry Sagen?" Donny questioned.

"He wants the person who killed Que dead. I don't have any other choice. I have to protect Sage," Nora explained.

They exchanged glances, each person weighing the risks and consequences of getting involved in a potential war. None of them seemed eager to step into the midst of the brewing conflict.

"You know what, none of you really have a choice in the matter," Nora declared. "You have to help me."

Mylan narrowed his eyes at Nora. "What the hell is that supposed to mean?"

"If I don't bring someone to Harry, all of us, including Sage and Avery, are as good as dead. Harry has his people following all of you. I saw the pictures."

At that moment, everyone realized the danger they were in. Mylan's eyes widened, darting around the surroundings with a heightened intensity. The calmness that once occupied his gaze was replaced by a rapid flickering, as if he was scanning for any signs of potential threat. "Did they follow us here?"

"I don't know. Maybe," she responded, her brows furrowing slightly and her tone lacking its usual confidence.

Mylan's eyes blazed with a fiery, fixed accusingly on Nora, as he shouted, "Damn it! This is exactly what I've been warning you about. You never think things through. You knew Harry had us under surveillance, and yet you gathered us all in one place. A perfect setup for him to wipe us out."

Nora's face paled as she realized the gravity of her actions. Her voice trembled with regret as she stammered, "I... I... I didn't think this through."

Sarah's eyes narrowed, her lips pressed into a thin line as her words sliced through the tense air. "You never do. Now we're all just sitting ducks."

"Listen, we can go back and forth about this or figure out what the hell to do." Warren's voice broke through the escalated tension, cutting through the blame and frustration that hung heavy in the air.

"We need to give him Kamari," Donny interjected.

Mylan nodded as he acknowledged Donny's suggestion. "Harry will not stop until he finds out who did this. Donny's right. Our best bet is to give him Kamari."

They all found themselves in agreement, except for Sarah, who voiced her concerns. "Hold on, everyone. Have you all really considered the consequences of setting up this woman? We know nothing about her or the potential repercussions. She could have friends or family who would come after us. This plan is reckless and dangerous."

"Well then, we need to find out everything we need to know about this Kamari chick. In the meantime, I will let Harry know that I have some leads to buy some time," Nora spoke with determination.

Mylan and Sarah shared a worried look before hurrying to their car and driving away. Donny followed suit, sensing the seriousness of the situation. Nora and Warren were left standing there, the weight of the moment sinking in. Warren gazed at Nora, "I may not have been there for her like I wish I was, but I'll do anything and everything to protect my daughter," Warren declared.

Chapter 22

Deceptions

Sage and Kamari sat in a car outside the hospital. Kamari leaned in close, her voice barely above a whisper. "This is your last chance to get her when no one is around. Just go in and stick her with his needle, and she'll be done," Kamari assured, her eyes gleamed with malice.

"What's in it?" Sage questioned, her brows furrowed slightly.

Kamari's lips curled into a sinister smile. "Fentanyl," she whispered, her voice dripping with a dangerous allure.

Kamari's words hit Sage like a punch to the gut. Her body tensed, and a flicker of panic flashed across her face. She leaned back, creating a physical distance between herself and Kamari. "Are you serious? I can't give her this."

"It's a hospital. Someone could have accidentally given it to her. Calm down." Kamari said.

Sage put on sunglasses and pulled her hoodie over her head, concealing her identity. Dressed in dark attire, she entered the hospital with a purposeful stride. Knowing the room number, she carefully navigated the corridors, blending in with the busy surroundings. As she approached the elevator, her heart skipped a beat when a uniformed police officer emerged from its confines.

Sage quickly diverted her gaze, pretending to search for something in her surroundings, waiting for the officer to disappear. Once the coast was clear, she swiftly entered the elevator, her nerves tingling with a mix of anticipation and fear.

Sage's heart thumped in her chest as she approached the room. She paused for a moment, taking a deep breath to steady herself before reaching for the doorknob. With a careful twist, she opened the door, revealing the girl inside, her back turned. Sage lowered her hoodie and removed her sunglasses, revealing her face.

As the girl turned around and locked eyes with Sage, her body tensed. The color drained from her face, and her lips quivered slightly as she took in the unexpected presence before her. "Why are you here?" she asked, her voice trembled.

Sage's smirk widened. Without hesitation, she swiftly closed the distance between them. As her eyes caught sight of the girl's hand inching towards the call button. With a forceful grip, Sage grabbed hold of the girl's hand, preventing her from reaching the call button. "Oh no, no, we can't have that," she taunted.

"I got my parents to drop the charges," she pleaded, her voice quivered. "I swear, I won't say shit about you being here. Please, don't hurt me. I'm outta here tomorrow. I'll do whatever you need, no questions asked. You ain't gotta go through with this."

"I guess you're finally getting a taste of that hospital life, huh? Ain't so pleasant, is it?" Sage hissed, her voice dripped with disdain. Concealing the syringe in her pocket, she patiently bided her time, waiting for the perfect moment to strike.

"You got this all wrong. She's been lying to you."

"What the hell are you talking about? Who's lying to me?" Sage's eyebrows furrowed, her forehead creased with lines of confusion. Her eyes narrowed, searching for answers, while her lips formed a slight frown.

"Chuckie, or should I say Kamari? She's not really your friend," she said.

Sage's eyes widened, and her brows furrowed. "You think that's going to stop me from killing you?"

"I'm telling you the truth. She told us to jump you," she admitted.

Sage continued to listen.

"She knew who you were before you stepped foot in the park and when you didn't take the bait about her protecting you from us, she made us jump you. Then she had you kill my homegirl. She is setting you up. Can't you see that?"

Sage's restless movements reflected her inner turmoil as she paced back and forth, her steps quick and agitated. The lines on her forehead deepened, and her hands clenched into fists. "She wouldn't do that to me. She loves me like a sister."

The girl sighed, "Kamari doesn't love anybody but herself. She's always been like that ever since we were kids."

Sage leaned forward slightly, as she asked, "How did you and Kamari meet?"

"She was my foster sister before I was adopted."

Sage shook her head. "That's not true. She lived with grand-mother after her parents died."

"Parents? Her mother walked out on her and her father. She never even knew her mom, and her grandmother never cared for her. Her father got killed in a home invasion, and that's when she ended up in the system," the girl explained, her voice tinged with sadness. She wiped away a tear from her face. "Everything she told you was a lie, and if I were you, I'd run."

Sage felt a heavy blow as her words sank in. Her heart raced, and she struggled to catch her breath. The truth overwhelmed her, leaving her stunned.

Moments later, Sage silently returned to the car. Her face remained devoid of any emotion, her features stoic and unmoving. Her eyes, usually filled with vibrancy and life, now seemed hollow, as if a spark within her had been extinguished. Kamari eagerly looked at her, awaiting confirmation. "Is it done?" she asked, anticipation clear in her voice.

Sage's grin stretched across her face, but it held no trace of joy or satisfaction. It was a chilling smile, one that seemed to reveal a darkness that had consumed her. "She won't be a problem anymore."

Kamari's excitement radiated through her as she tapped Sage's back, but Sage didn't respond with the same enthusiasm. She simply nodded. Her expression remained detached. "That's what the fuck I'm talking about."

"I guess there's just one more person left," Sage said, her gaze fixed on Kamari.

Kamari smiled, her eyes locked with Sage's. "Are you ready for this? Once you do it, there's no turning back," she explained.

"It's time that my mother pays for what she's done."

Kamari's laughter filled the car as she shifted into drive and sped away, leaving behind a trail of uncertainty and darkness.

Chapter 23

Darkness

It was nearly 1 a.m. when Sage stealthily entered the condo, expecting everyone to be asleep. However, to her surprise, the living room was filled with a tense atmosphere. Sarah's eyes were puffy and red, showing recent tears, while Nora's agitated pacing reflected her anxiety. Mylan was engrossed in a flurry of phone calls, his brows furrowed with concern. Sage's heart sank as she processed the scene before her.

"Oh, my god. Is Avery with you?" Sarah's desperate question pierced through the silence.

Sage scanned the room, her eyes widening as she took in the palpable panic that gripped everyone. "No, she isn't. What's going on?"

"Avery is missing. When I went to pick her up from school, she wasn't there. I assumed you were with her, considering you weren't home either. So, where were you? And why are you just getting home now?" Nora questioned.

Sage opened her mouth to respond, but Nora interrupted her, "And don't you dare tell me you were with that Kamari girl."

Sage quickly responded, "No, I wasn't with Kamari, I swear."

Nora asked Sage if she knew any of Avery's friends. It dawned on Sage that she hadn't spoken to Avery in a long time. Their rooms had been right across from each other, yet she never stepped inside. She had been so consumed by her own troubles that she neglected to see how Avery was doing.

Sage went to Avery's room and searched through her belongings, hoping to find a clue about her whereabouts. As she opened Avery's laptop, the Amtrak schedule to Buffalo appeared on the screen. Sage called out for Nora, and together, they hastily put on their jackets and headed towards the door. As they opened the door to leave, they were taken aback to find Avery standing in the doorway, holding her key in hand.

"Oh my god," Nora exhaled. "Avery, what the hell? Where were you?"

Avery walked into the condo and asked, "What's wrong with y'all?" while rolling her eyes.

Nora grabbed her by the collar, but Mylan quickly intervened, pulled her away, and gently pushed Nora to the side.

"Were you trying to go to Buffalo?" Mylan asked with a concerned tone.

Avery crossed her arms and rolled her eyes. "Why do you even care? It's none of your business," she said.

Nora's voice surged with anger, and her jaw clenched tightly. "Watch your mouth, little girl."

"I don't know why y'all tripping. I came back," Avery retorted casually, grabbing a water bottle from the fridge.

"You've got to be kidding me! It's one in the morning, and you're just showing up, and you don't know why we're tripping out?" Nora exclaimed.

"Yeah, why the hell are y'all tripping? It's not like you notice me when I'm here," Avery snapped.

"What is that supposed to mean?" Nora asked.

Avery's voice trembled with pent-up emotion as she continued, "Everything is about Sage. Sage skipping school, beating up people, hanging with the wrong crowd." She slammed the water bottle on the table. "Y'all don't give a damn about me."

In that moment, it dawned on Nora that they had all been too caught up dealing with Sage's drama to pay enough attention to Avery's struggles. She could see the truth in Avery's words, and it hit her hard. They'd been neglecting her without even realizing it. Nora felt a weight of guilt on her shoulders and knew they had to step up as a family, to have each other's backs and not let anyone feel left out or ignored. "Yes we do," Nora explained. "We all care about you."

Avery's voice trembled, "I bet y'all didn't even know I'm failing all my classes. I might have to repeat the 7th grade, but I don't even care," she said, as she crossed her arms.

"What was your plan? Go back to Buffalo and live with your aunt Matty," Mylan questioned.

"I damn well planned it that way. I hate this hellhole, and I'd rather be anywhere else but here," Avery yelled.

"It's not that bad," Sage chimed in, offering a reassuring hand on Avery's shoulder.

Avery brushed her off. "That's easy for you to say. You have a bunch of friends. All I get is people calling me white girl every day, but you wouldn't know anything about what's going on with me because you're too busy being a crackhead."

All eyes darted at Sage, and her palms turned sweaty as beads of sweat dripped down her forehead. She let out a nervous laugh. "What are you even talking about? I don't do drugs. Are you crazy?"

"Oh, you don't. Huh?" Avery stormed into Sage's room, her emotions running high. The room turned into a whirlwind of chaos as Avery tore through everything. Sage's heart raced like it was on a racetrack, her mind trying to figure a way out of this mess, but her words were stuck in her throat.

Nora and Mylan rushed in, trying to pull the two apart. Mylan kept Sage at bay while Nora attempted to reason with

Avery. "Avery, calm down. What the hell is wrong with you?" Nora screamed.

Avery then found what she was looking for. A hidden stash of that white powder. Sage clenched her fists and her body tensed up. Her gaze wavered between the bag of cocaine and Avery, her mind racing with thoughts and regrets.

Nora's eyes moved from Avery to Sage. "Avery, go to your room. We will talk about this in the morning," she demanded, gesturing towards the door. Nora handed the stash of cocaine to Sarah and asked her to flush it down the toilet.

"Are you doing drugs?" Nora questioned.

Sage sat on the bed with her head down. "It was only a few times," she admitted.

Nora took a seat at Sage's desk while Mylan stood. She took a deep breath before speaking again. "I'm not mad at you."

Sage looked up and Mylan narrowed his eyes at Nora, as they were both shocked at her response. "You're not mad?" Sage asked.

"How can I be mad at you when everything that has happened in the past year is because of me?" Nora sat beside Sage and held her hand. "I would rather you be selling than using, but that's beside the point."

Mylan playfully kicked Nora's foot. "Life is tough, but drugs aren't the answer, Sage. You can die from this shit, especially if you don't know where it's coming from. Speaking of where it came from. Who gave it to you?"

Sage darted her eyes between Mylan and Nora. "Kamari."

"Did she tell you to kill Que?" Mylan questioned.

Sage looked at him in shock that he knew what she had done. She explained what happened with Que and the girl she killed in the warehouse. Sage continued to confess what happened at the hospital and revealed that Kamari was in a foster home before she turned 18.

Mylan and Nora stood over her as they progressed to what she had told them. "We are fucked," Nora said. "The boy that you killed was the stepson of Harry Segan and he wants me to bring the killer to him and if I don't, he will kill all of us."

* * *

Seated with her back to the door, Avery's soft whimpers echoed through the hallway. Nora peeked her head in and asked if she could join her. Receiving a nod in response, Nora entered the room.

Nora settled down beside her, reached out to place her hand on Avery's, but Avery withdrew her hand. With a deep breath, Nora spoke. "Avery, I'm truly sorry. My attention has been so consumed by your sister that I completely overlooked checking in on you."

Avery shrugged her shoulders dismissively, her voice carrying a hint of resignation. "Just the usual, being overlooked, like always."

The weight of Avery's words tugged at Nora's heart, which caused a pang of sorrow. "I never meant to make you feel that way."

"You know what's even worse?" Avery's youthful voice carried a tinge of bitterness as she looked at her mother. "Losing my dad, and then seeing Sage get all the attention, even though she's not even his actual daughter."

Nora tried to respond, but her words caught in her throat.

Avery pressed on, "You all act like I'm too young to know anything, like I can't handle the truth. But I see and hear everything. When I found out what you did to daddy, I didn't freak out. I didn't turn to drugs or kill anyone. I dealt with it on my own."

Nora's voice softened as she replied, "You shouldn't have had to handle that alone. I should have been there for you."

Avery's voice wavered as she rose to her feet. Her eyes held a blend of emotions. "I had to handle it alone, 'cause none of you were there for me. You're all stuck in anger, but that's not who I am. Daddy didn't raise me to be like this."

"I understand." Nora rose to her feet, her tone softer now. She extended a hand toward Avery, but Avery evaded the gesture once more.

"Do you, Mom? Do you really understand? Because I don't think you do." she retreated to the other side of the room.

"I've always seen you as my smart little girl. You rarely ever needed anything. You've always been so independent," Nora explained.

"My independence doesn't negate the fact that I'm still a kid and I need a shoulder to cry on," Avery said. "My dad is gone, and it's hard not having anyone to talk to about him."

"You're right. You're still a little girl, and I know I haven't been there for you like I should have been," Nora admitted, her voice tinged with regret. "It's hard to be the one you turn to for comfort when I'm the one who caused you so much pain."

Avery walked towards Nora, her voice soft but firm. "That's your guilt to carry, not mine."

Nora took a deep breath. Her eyes met Avery's. "You're right, Avery. I'm the one who has to carry that guilt, and I will. But I also want to be here for you, to support you, and to be the mother you need."

Avery looked at Nora, her expression still holding a mix of hurt and uncertainty. "I don't hate you," she began softly, "but trust is earned. A simple apology won't fix it and if I ever want to talk about Dad, no matter how guilty you feel, listen."

Nora nodded. "I respect that, Avery. I'm here whenever you're ready to talk, and I'll do my best to earn back your trust.

Just remember, I love you more than anything." She reached out, her hand extended for a hug.

Avery looked at Nora for a moment. She took a deep breath and then stepped into the embrace, as she allowed herself to be enveloped in her mother's arms.

* * *

The following morning, a loud, authoritative knock echoed through the condo. Nora had stayed the night, so she was still there when the door swung open, revealing Detective Douglas and Detective Matthew standing side by side. The sound of the knock drew everyone's attention, and they hurried to the entrance to see what was happening.

"How can we help you, detective?" Sarah asked politely.

"We have some questions for Sage Woods. May we sit?" Douglas asked.

Sarah exchanged glances with Mylan and Nora, seeking their approval before allowing them in. Mylan gave a subtle nod, signaling it was alright. Nora and Sage settled on the sofa, while Sarah opted for the rocking chair, and Mylan remained standing. Avery lingered in the hallway, eavesdropping on the conversation. "What is this about?" Nora inquired.

"Kelsey Moore was killed this morning right when she was about to be released from the hospital. I thought you might want to know," Matthew stated, his expression serious.

Sage furrowed her brows, her body tense with confusion. "Kelsey? I don't know who that is," she said, her voice wavered as she spoke.

"The girl that she put in the hospital. She was being released this morning and when her nurse went to check on her, she was found with a syringe in her neck," detective Matthew explained.

Sage's eyes widened in disbelief. Her jaw dropped slightly as she blurted out, "What?" The shock was unmistakable in her expression. Her body tensed up with the unexpected news.

Detective Douglas' gaze intensified, his eyes locked onto Sage as he stated, "A lethal amount of fentanyl was found in that syringe. It killed her instantly." He then continued with a stern tone, "I would like to know where you were between the hours of 7 pm and 12 o'clock am."

Sage's voice wavered slightly as she lied, "I was with my friend Tegan until like 8, and then I was home around 9."

Nora placed her arm around Sage's shoulder in support, showing her agreement.

Douglas raised an eyebrow. "Interesting," he said. "After reviewing the footage around 7:00 pm, we noticed someone dressed in all black. That person deliberately kept their head down, avoiding the camera."

"What does this have to do with my daughter?" Nora demanded. "And you know what? Is she under arrest?"

Detective Matthew sighed. "As of now, she's not under arrest, but we need to investigate further. The timing and the circumstances are quite suspicious. We just want to sort this out." He glanced at Sage with a serious expression.

Nora stood up and swung the door open, gesturing for the detectives to leave. Both Douglas and Matthew got up to exit. "If I were you, I wouldn't plan on leaving town anytime soon," Matthew warned, directing his statement at Sage.

Nora closed the door behind them, and her gaze swept across everyone in the room. "Kamari has to go," she asserted firmly. Feeling a sense of desperation to protect her daughter, Nora contemplated a tough decision. She couldn't bear the thought of Sage following a dangerous path like she did. In her mind, the only way to protect her was by blaming someone else.

Sage stood, taking a cautious step back. "Kamari and I made a list of people we wanted revenge on," she admitted. "And the last person on the list... is you." Her eyes locked firmly onto Nora's. Her eyes fell to the ground with her shoulders slumped as a wave of guilt washed over her.

"Then we use that to our advantage," Mylan added.

Avery's eyes widened, and her mouth hung open in utter disbelief. The shock was clear on her face, her features frozen. She looked from Sage to their mother, unable to process the gravity of the situation. Tears welled up in her eyes. "Dad would have never wanted this for us." With a heavy heart, she turned away and rushed to her room.

Chapter 24

Shadowed

"You sure you want to do this? I don't want you to have to choose between me and your family," Nora asked as she gazed up at Luke.

He stared at her intensely. "Harry has proven to me time and time again that all he cares about is his precious casino. Family was the furthest thing from his mind. So, there is no choice that needs to be made." He caressed her cheek. "Because I'll always choose you."

They quickly separated once they heard Harry's men signaling for Nora to come to his office. She followed behind them and she shared a glance with Luke before disappearing through the crowd of people in the casino.

Harry smiled as Nora entered his office. "This must be good news." He drank a glass of whiskey and swallowed hard. "What do you have for me?"

"The person who killed Que goes by the name Chuckie," Nora said.

Harry stood and looked as if he was thinking. "What do you know about this Chuckie person?"

"Apparently Que owed Chuckie some money and when he didn't pay it, she shot him. She is in her early 20s, African-

Harry cut her off before she could finish. "Did you just say she? As in a woman?" he said, shocked.

Nora shook her head yes.

Harry looked at her with anger in his eyes. "I want you to bring her to me."

* * *

While Sage was lost in thought leaving school, Kamari grabbed her arm and led her to the car, insisting they talk. Without a word, Kamari drove off, steering them to a secluded area where they could speak in private.

"What's going on?" Sage inquired, trying her best not to show the fear creeping into her. Her face remained composed, though her heart raced.

"Bitch, you lied to me. You said you killed her and you didn't. Of course, I had to finish the job." Kamari yelled.

"You don't trust me," Sage said, as she attempted to deflect the blame.

Kamari grabbed her by the neck, fury in her eyes. "Don't play me, bitch. After everything I did for you, why did you lie to me?" she seethed.

Sage's voice trembled as she confessed, "I didn't want to get caught. As I was going to her room, and a nurse went in there, and I couldn't just wait around. I already looked suspicious, wearing all fucking black. I couldn't go through with it, and I lied to you because... because I didn't want you to think that I was useless." Her eyes flickered.

Kamari's grip on Sage's neck loosened, her anger giving way to hurt and vulnerability. "You should have just said that. You're the last person I thought would lie to me," she admitted.

A single tear escaped her eye. "My parents used to lie to me, and it makes me angry." As quickly as the tears appeared, her eyes hardened with a menacing look. "You're my family, and I don't want you to ever lie to me again," she warned.

Sage swallowed hard. "I promise I won't." Although a part of her wanted to feel sorry for Kamari, she couldn't ignore all the lies and deception she had witnessed. Sage knew she had to stay alert and protect herself from getting tangled in Kamari's dangerous web.

Kamari reached into the backseat of her car, pulling out a gun. "Look what I got," she said, her voice cold.

Sage's voice was firm, and her eyes narrowed. "Is that the gun that Que was shot with? I thought you got rid of it and the clothes."

Kamari's voice remained cold and calculated as she spoke. "I got rid of the clothes, but I keep this in my truck. This is from your first kill. It's only right that we use this for Nora," she replied. "So, how can we get her alone?"

Sage felt uneasy as Kamari quickly shifted the focus to Nora, making her wonder if Kamari was obsessed with her mother. "Usually after work, she goes to this parking lot in the mall on level 4. Something about her childhood. I don't freaking know," Sage said, playing along with Kamari's plan despite her discomfort.

Kamari grinned. "That's perfect. Tomorrow night we'll do it. After that, you'll finally be free, and we'll live happily ever after. Just me and you," Kamari said, her voice filled with a sinister excitement.

Sage kept her fear hidden, not daring to say anything in response to Kamari's chilling words.

* * *

Later that day, Sage found herself confined to the cold, sterile walls of the interrogation room. Sage appeared calm, but her trembling knee said otherwise. She looked up as detective Douglas and Matthew entered the room. "What brings you here?" Matthew inquired, his tone neutral yet observant.

Sage leaned forward, her eyes locking onto the detective's. "If I tell y'all everything, I expect full immunity," she demanded.

Matthew and Douglas exchanged glances, their expressions unreadable. "That depends on the extent of your involvement in whatever you're about to reveal," Matthew replied, his tone cautious.

Sage rose from her seat, a sense of urgency in her movements. "I need more than that. I want full immunity, no matter what I say," she insisted, her voice firm.

"Fine, fine. Please have a seat," Douglas responded. "Does your mother know you're here?" he asked.

Sage carefully settled back in the seat, threw a quick shake of her head to signify her mother didn't know she was there.

"Well, we can't speak to you without a parent or lawyer present," Douglas said.

Matthew nudged him and whispered, "What the fuck are you doing?"

Sage defiantly crossed her arms as she looked determined. "I'm 16, and I know my rights. Give me the document guaranteeing full immunity, and then I'll tell you everything you need to know."

An hour passed before Mathew, and Douglas returned to the room with the document. Sage carefully read every word before taking the pen and signing it. She insisted on receiving a copy for herself before saying anything. Once she had the copy in hand, she was finally ready to speak.

Matthew inquired, "Who killed Kelsey Moore?"

Sage took a deep breath and leaned back in the chair. "Her name is Kamari, but she goes by the name... Chuckie," she revealed. "And that's not the only person she killed."

Matthew and Douglas exchanged glances; their interest piqued by Sage's revelation. They leaned in attentively, ready to hear more.

Chapter 25

Fractured

Nora, Mylan, Warren, and Donny gathered in the living room of the condo. "How are you so sure this is going to work?" Warren questioned Nora.

She shot him a narrowed-eyed look. "My plans never flop," she retorted.

"No, they don't," Warren replied.

As they huddled, devising their strategy, Sage stormed into the condo. A scowl etched across her face as her gaze fell on Warren. "Seriously?" she erupted. "What the hell is he doing here?"

Nora swiftly rose from her seat and guided Sage toward her room. Sage's bag landed on the floor with a thud. Inside the room, Sage's frustration boiled over. "I can't believe you'd bring him here. What were you thinking?" she spat out..

"First off, lower your tone," Nora replied firmly. "The only reason he's here is because we need all the people we can get."

Sage flopped down on her bed, her back turned to Nora. "I ... I just don't want him around," Sage said. Her knee bounced up and down in a nervous rhythm.

"I'll ask him to leave," Nora said.

Sage let out an exasperated sigh, rolling her eyes and shaking her head in frustration.

"I am trying to make you feel comfortable, so what is with the attitude?"

Sage's voice rose to a scream, anger evident in her tone. "I don't want you to make me feel comfortable. All I want you to do is talk to me and actually listen. I need to express how I feel. Not everything can be fixed with a snap of your fingers or a bullet from a gun."

Nora settled into the chair opposite Sage, their eyes locked in a steady gaze.

Sage inhaled deeply, mustering her courage. "I've been scared to tell you I feel really sad."

"Why would you be scared to tell me that?"

"Because you're the reason I feel this way. I couldn't tell you because you're always so aggressive and confrontational. It's like you're only concerned about yourself and you never see your own mistakes."

Nora found herself speechless, unable to respond.

Sage's voice trembled as she poured out her feelings. "Since Daddy was killed, everything has changed. I've changed. We're not the same anymore." She hesitated, her words hanging in the air. "And before you turned yourself in, you promised to tell me who you really are. So, who are you, Nora?"

Nora's voice quivered as she opened up. "I was a bad person, and I did terrible things. Even though I'm an adult with children, I'm still trying to figure out who I really am. But one thing is certain: I don't want to be a careless mother. My actions might have said otherwise, but I'm striving to make things right. I'll do anything to protect you and Avery."

Sage let out a sigh as she rose from the bed. "That might sound nice, but it's just not enough for me. You lied to me about who I am for half my life."

"You're still Sage Woods. It doesn't matter who your biological father is. That will never change. You're smart, strong, funny, and beautiful. That's who you are," Nora assured her.

"But what about the things I've done? The people I've hurt. It's like I'm becoming you, and I don't like how it feels," Sage confessed.

Nora gently placed her hands on Sage's shoulders. "You're better than me. My actions were selfish. But what you've done, it was manipulation by that bitch. She made you believe that hurting others was the only way to deal with your pain. But I'm here to tell you, it's not. You're better than that."

Sage wiped her damp eyes with her palm. "If you need Warren here to help, I'm okay with it. But I don't want to see him, so I'll stay in my room," she said as she settled back onto the bed.

"When this is all over, I think we should all go to family therapy. That's if the police don't arrest us first," Sage said, a faint smirk appeared on her lips.

"Yeah, because we all messed up in the head," Nora chuckled as she pulled Sage into a comforting embrace.

Chapter 26

Twisted

Sage and Kamari were parked in a car with the lights off, blending into the vast parking lot of the nearly empty mall. The night was falling, and the remaining few cars hinted that the mall's closing time was approaching. Kamari's fingers drummed on the dashboard, her irritated sigh breaking the silence. "You said she'd be here by now," she grumbled, her impatience etched across her face.

"She's on her way, calm down," Sage reassured. Her knee bounced as she scanned the parking lot.

Kamari narrowed her eyes at Sage, her expression tinged with suspicion, as she retrieved her gun and placed it on her lap.

A sudden burst of headlights sliced through the darkness, illuminating the parking lot as a car came to a halt. "There she is," Sage whispered, her breath hitching.

Kamari and Sage observed as Nora stepped out of her car and strolled towards the edge of the parking lot. Leaning against the railing, she took a drag from her blunt and gazed out at the street.

"You ready?" Kamari inquired, as she pulled back the gun's slide.

Sage's throat tightened, and she gave a shaky nod in response.

Kamari exited the car with a silent door closure, and Sage followed suit, their tense footsteps echoing on the pavement. They advanced side by side, guns leveled at Nora, who was standing by the balcony railing, her back to them. With a strained voice, Kamari called out, "Yo, Mercy."

Nora spun around, her eyes widening in shock as she locked onto the guns aimed at her. "What the hell? Sage, put that damn gun down!"

Sage stayed silent, the weight of the situation heavy in her chest as she held the gun steady at Nora. Her heart pounded in her ears, robbing her of words.

Nora's eyes locked onto Kamari's, betrayal flashed across her face. The air around them seemed to thicken as the truth hung between them. "You turned my daughter against me?" Nora's voice trembled

"Now she's your daughter? Was she even your daughter when you spent all those years lying to her? And what about when you took my father's life?" The words tumbled out of Kamari's mouth. "What about when you killed her father?" she quickly repeated. "All I did was help Sage find her strength because you took it from her."

Kamari's gaze shifted to Sage, her expression intense. "Finish this, Sage!"

Sage stood frozen, her eyes wide like a deer caught in headlights. Beads of sweat formed on her forehead, tracing a path down her trembling face. Her breaths grew heavier, the sound almost echoing.

Kamari whispered, "Think about that life you lost in Buffalo, the moments you shared with Henry. She stole it all from you."

A single tear escaped Sage's eye. She shifted her gaze from Kamari to Nora, their eyes locked.

"Don't listen to her, Sage. The bitch is insane!" Nora yelled.

Kamari's eyes blazed with rage, her grip on the gun tightening. "You haven't seen crazy yet," she hissed, her voice laced with fury. "Shoot her, now!" Her command echoed through the air, thick with menace.

The metallic click of the barrel being pulled back reverberated in Kamari's ears. She turned her head to find a gun pointed right at her. "You weak bitch. I should have known your punk ass couldn't go through with it," Kamari sneered, her voice dripping with contempt. She shifted her gaze to Nora and let out a mocking laugh. "You bitches set me up."

Sage's brow furrowed, and her eyes widened in confusion as she looked at Kamari, trying to make sense of her words, "I never told you my father's name."

"Yes, you did. You just don't remember," Kamari insisted, a smug smile playing on her lips. "You're confused because she's twisting your mind and trying to put you against me. But don't forget, I'm the only one who loves and cares about you. We're family."

"Sage, shoot that crazy bitch," Nora screamed.

Sage's shock was palpable as she pulled the trigger, and nothing happened. Kamari's laughter cut through the tense air. "Did you really think I'd give you a loaded gun?" She gripped Sage's collar. The gun dropped from Sage's hand as she attempted to dash toward Nora.

Nora pulled out her gun. "Let her go before-

"Before you what?" Kamari interjected, her voice sharp as she screamed. "I've got a gun to her head. You shoot me, I shoot her. Drop the fucking gun and kick it over to me. Now!"

Sage's eyes widened and trembled as her lips revealed the turmoil within her. She looked at her mother, hoping for a way out, just as Nora dropped the gun and kicked it over to Kamari.

Kamari holstered her gun and grabbed Nora's weapon. "Now, I'm driving out of here with your daughter, and you'll never lay eyes on her again."

"Your beef is with me for whatever reason. So they take me and let her go," Nora pleaded.

"Oh, no. That would be too simple," Kamari taunted. "I've heard that Harry Segan is hunting down Que's killer. It's only fitting that I deliver her to him."

Kamari brandished the gun, pressing it against Sage's back, coercing her into the car. A swift strike of the gun's butt left Sage unconscious, slumped in the seat. Kamari hopped into the driver's seat and sped away.

Nora got into her car and sped away. She dialed Warren's number and shouted into the phone, "She took Sage! She took Sage!"

Warren's voice crackled through the car's speaker, "What the hell do you mean she took Sage?"

"Are you not fucking hearing me?" Nora's voice cracked with desperation. "Something ain't right with that girl. She spoke to me like she knew me. That I killed Henry. She told Sage that she loved her more than me and she was her family."

Nora swerved through traffic, trying to keep up with Kamari, but she had lost them.

"What is that supposed to mean?" Warren questioned.

"I don't freaking know. The bitch is obsessed with Sage's father being killed. Like I killed her-" Nora abruptly halted her words, a sudden realization crossing her mind about Kamari's true identity.

"We had a fucking plan, Nora." Warren yelled.

"Screw the plan. Get Donny and meet me at the Casino. I'll contact Mylan and Luke," Nora barked into the phone before cutting off the call, her gaze locked on the road ahead.

Chapter 27

Inferno

Kamari's footsteps echoed in the confined space as Sage regained awareness. Her surroundings came into focus, a dim lit basement, with Kamari paced back and forth. The room contained nothing more than the solitary chair Sage was in and an empty table.

"Oh, you're finally awake," Kamari grimaced.

Sage struggled against the restraints of the chair. "What the hell is this? Where are we?"

Kamari's voice was a mix of anger and hurt as she spoke. "You called me your big sister. Why would you choose Nora over me? I did everything for you. I kept you safe." She waved the gun around, her grip shaky.

Sage's gaze hardened, her response sharp. "You didn't keep me safe. You made those girls attack me. Freaking weirdo."

The cold metal of the gun pressed against Sage's skin, just below her chin, as Kamari's grip tightened.. "I did you a favor.

You needed me. You just couldn't see it yet, so I did what I had to do, and you came running like clockwork."

"Fuck you!" Sage's voice trembled.

Kamari's lips curled into a sinister grin, her eyes glinting with a mix of amusement and malice. "Such a potty mouth," she taunted, her tone mocking. "What was her excuse about what she did to you?

Sage clenched her fists, her knuckles turning white, but she remained silent.

Kamari's patience wore thin. Her voice escalated to a shout. "Tell me!" she demanded. Her finger trembled as she pointed the gun.

Sage's gaze bore into Kamari's. She shook her head, refusing to speak.

Kamari's laughter had an edge of madness to it, a chilling sound that echoed in the dimly lit, damp basement "You don't have to answer me because whatever she said was a load of bull and you fell for it," she sneered. Her posture exuded arrogance as if she held all the power in the room. "I tried to help you. I even shot Cylus."

The room was heavy with tension, the stale air carried the weight of their confrontation.

"That was you? Sage questioned. "He could have died. What the hell is wrong with you?"

"He was distracting you. I did what I needed to do. He's lucky he ain't dead. You lucky I didn't shoot you."

Sage's eyes were red from her tears. She choked on her words, "Why didn't you?"

Kamari grinned. "I needed you for the grand finale." She glanced up, her ears catching the sound of footsteps approaching. "And so it begins."

Harry sauntered in, followed by four men, among them Luke. "Well, well," his voice resonated, carrying an air of authority. "Looks like we've got the infamous young lady here, the one causing all the fuss."

Sage's gaze rose to meet the man that stood before her. A surge of anger coursed through her veins, making her feel as though her skin might burst into flames. Her attention remained locked on Kamari, who extended her hand to Harry with a confident grin.

One man handed Kamari a duffle bag. Sage's eyes narrowed, her fists clenched, and her teeth ground together. Kamari leaned in, her breath close to Sage's ear, sending a shiver down her spine. "I'll see you on the other side." With a final, knowing glance, Kamari turned and walked away, leaving Sage with a gnawing uncertainty about what lay ahead.

"Sweetie, huh?" Harry's fingers brushed against Sage's cheek. His gaze shifted briefly to his men before he issued a command. "Open my bag."

Sage's eyes were fixed on the bag as it was placed on the table. Her heart raced. Inside was an array of menacing tools, instruments designed for causing pain. A thin sheen of sweat formed on her forehead, her struggle against the restraints intensifying as desperation set in.

"I'm going to kill you now, but I'll take my time. I want to enjoy this." Harry's smile widened. His tone carried a chilling sound of sadistic pleasure.

* * *

Nora, Mylan, Warren, and Donny entered the bustling casino. "I got a text from Luke. They have her in the basement," Nora informed the group, her voice tense with urgency.

"We need to get these people out. No need for any dead bodies," Warren asserted.

Donny's eyes scanned the surroundings and locked onto the fire alarms. He relayed his plan to Nora and Mylan. Finding Sage was their priority, while he and Warren would focus on clearing the area. With a nod, they divided.

Nora and Mylan navigated their way through the bustling casino, catching the attention of vigilant security guards who surrounded them. The guards' stern expressions mirrored their firm stance. "You're not allowed in the building," the guard stated, his voice an authoritative reminder.

Nora met his gaze with a determined look. "Harry told me I could pick up my last check. I don't have time for this," she countered. The noise of the casino patrons and the flashing lights of slot machines added to the tense atmosphere.

As the guards exchanged glances, a sudden gunshot shattered the tense silence. The bullet found its target with deadly precision, taking down one guard in a spray of blood, and chaos ensued. Simultaneously, the shrill sound of the fire alarm pierced the air, mingling with the panicked cries of casino-goers.

Amid the pandemonium, people scattered in every direction, seeking cover from the ongoing gunfire. The rhythmic popping of bullets and the intermittent screams intensified the sense of terror. Nora's attention sharpened as she spotted Kamari and returned fire in her direction. She made a swift hand gesture to Mylan and directed him to flank Kamari from the other side of the casino, hoping to catch her off guard.

On the opposite end of the casino floor, Donny and Warren's voices rose above the chaos, their urgent screams urged everyone to evacuate. People panicked as they formed a chaotic jumble of bodies, their faces etched with desperation as they scrambled and stumbled over each other, trying to escape the unfolding turmoil.

The wailing fire alarm, blaring slot machines, and echoing gunshots merged into a disoriented mix of noise, adding to the atmosphere of sheer mayhem.

From the dark basement, you could hear the escalating chaos from above. Harry's authoritative voice cut through the commotion and instructed Luke to investigate the disturbance. Luke abandoned the scene, leaving behind two guards, Sage still bound to the chair, and an restless Harry.

"Now, where were we?" Harry's voice held a sinister edge as he retrieved a gleaming, sharp implement resembling a knife.

"Please, listen to me. That girl is the one that killed Que. She lied to you," Sage pleaded.

"I find it hard to believe you. Why else would your mother drag her feet to tell me who killed my stepson? Obviously, to shield you," he chuckled darkly. "But I can't fault her for that. I'd do anything to safeguard my loved ones."

Harry positioned himself in front of her, his finger glided along the weapon. "This is a stiletto, a tiger tooth stiletto. It's named for its design resembling a tiger's teeth. This one's a favorite of mine."

Without hesitation, he drove the stiletto into Sage's right thigh, sending waves of agony through her body. Her screams echoed through the room as she writhed in the chair, tears streamed down her face. The crack of gunfire pierced the air. Luke appeared, eliminating both guards.

Harry's voice was thick with menace as he held the gun to Harry's head. "You're going to regret this," he said.

Luke's finger tightened on the trigger, and his uncle crumpled to his knees before collapsing. He wasted no time and rushed to untie Sage, as he improvised a makeshift bandage with his tie to staunch the blood from her thigh. She gritted her teeth against the pain and leaned on Luke, her arm draped around his shoulder for support. Every step was a struggle, the agony almost overwhelming, but Luke's determination never wavered. With careful effort, he guided her towards the exit.

In the main area of the casino, chaos still reigned as panicked people streamed out of the building. Amidst the frenzy, Donny, Warren, Nora, and Mylan engaged in a fierce exchange of gunfire with the guards and Kamari from various corners of the casino.

Donny's keen eyes spotted a direct route to reach Kamari, and he seized the opportunity, closing the distance. He pressed his gun to her head, his voice firm as he ordered her to put the gun down.

Kamari turned with a slow, deliberate movement, meeting Donny's gaze with defiance. The barrel of the gun was now pressed against her forehead, but her laughter erupted, echoing through the tumultuous surroundings. "Shoot me. I was waiting to die, anyway. Do it if you got the balls," she laughed.

"I know you're the one who shot Cylus," Donny said.

"Fuck the chit-chat. If you're tough, then pull the trigger and shoot me!" Kamari's voice rose to a piercing scream.

Donny squeezed the trigger, but the click of an empty chamber met his ears. His eyes widened with a mixture of terror and disbelief, his body frozen in the realization that his gun was empty.

"Say hi to my father for me?" Kamari's voice dripped with venom as she yanked the trigger. Donny's body convulsed and collapsed onto the ground. A pool of crimson rapidly formed around him.

Chapter 28

Redemption

Warren's anguished cry tore through the chaotic sounds of the casino. He surged to his feet, firing his gun in a desperate rage. A bullet found its mark on Kamari's shoulder, which caused her to retreat in pain and vanish into hiding. Warren rushed to Donny's side, sinking to his knees. Nora and Mylan hurried over, their faces a mix of concern and grief. Warren clung to Donny's lifeless form; tears streamed down his cheeks. His voice trembled with emotion as he vowed, "I'm going to kill her."

Nora's voice, urgent and steady, cut through the turmoil. "We need her alive."

Warren's eyes burned with a mixture of pain and seething rage. "I'm done. I'm fucking done," he declared, his voice trembled. He gazed down at Donny's lifeless form. He pulled the body closer, his arms wrapped tightly around him. In a soft, broken whisper, he choked out, "I'm sorry. I'm so sorry."

Luke and Sage approached; their own grief etched on their faces. Sage's scream pierced the air as she saw Donny's lifeless body cradled by Warren. Despite her own pain, she rushed to Donny's side, repeating the word "no" in a heart-wrenching chorus of denial.

Nora rose to her feet and embraced Luke, seeking comfort in his presence. "What happened?" she whispered, her voice heavy. In response, Luke met her gaze. His eyes conveyed the painful truth of the situation without uttering a single word. The weight of his unspoken explanation settled on Nora's heart as understanding dawned in her eyes.

After taking a quick survey of their surroundings, Nora's attention was drawn to the sudden cessation of gunfire. Her gaze swept across the scene, noting the fallen guards and the chaos that had come to a halt.

"Kamari, it's over!" Nora's voice cut through the tense air. "Come out, you crazy bitch! If you want me, come and face me!" Her words echoed through the chaotic aftermath. Nora's gaze scanned the surroundings, her eyes sharp and determined. "This was never about Sage," she continued, her voice cracked. "It was always between you and me. You're angry at me, I understand. I'm sorry!" Her admission hung heavy in the air, a confession laden with guilt and regret. "I'm sorry I killed our father," she confessed, her voice heavy with the weight of her past actions.

All heads turned upward, eyes widened in a collective shock. The confession hung heavy in the air.

Kamari stepped into view, her shoulder swathed in makeshift cloth, crimson seeping through the fabric. Despite the pain, she clutched a gun in her other hand and wore a twisted smile on her lips. "Hey sis," she drawled. "It's about time you connected the dots," she teased.

Warren rose, his body drenched in Donny's blood, and positioned himself beside Nora. Their eyes remained fixed on Kamari, a surge of memories flooding back to the night Mikey had died. The toll of time had altered Kamari, yet the turmoil still lived within her eyes, a perpetual flame of pain.

"What was your plan?" Nora's voice was steady, her gaze pierced as she confronted Kamari. "Get close to my daughter. Make her kill me."

Kamari's smirk held a mix of bitterness and satisfaction. "I mean, you've got it all figured out. Quite the detective, huh?" She let out a dry chuckle. "But killing you? Nah, that was never my first choice. You deserve to feel the agony I've felt all these years."

Nora's anger flared, her voice rising. "He was a monster, a rapist. I did the world a favor. I did you a favor."

Kamari's fury blazed, her words seething with resentment. "You did me a favor? You turned my life into a nightmare. I bounced from one damn foster home to another while you lived it up. You painted Mikey as a monster. What the hell does that make you?" Anger pulsed through her, obvious sweat running down her face.

Warren's voice trembled with remorse, each word carried the weight of his regret. His eyes were downcast, unable to meet the gaze of those around him. The pain in his tone was palpable. "We were kids. I know that can't change the past, but we're sorry."

Tears welled up in Kamari's eyes. "I was just five years old. He bled out in my arms. I can't erase that image from my mind."

"We want to make things right," Warren implored.

Kamari's anger erupted like a volcano. "Shut the fuck up!" she screamed, her finger tightening on the trigger. And then, the gunshot shattered the stillness, a sharp crack that seemed to reverberate through time.

Warren's world exploded in pain as the bullet tore through his arm, forcing him to collapse onto the floor. Nora's anguished scream filled the air as she watched. But Sage, fueled by adrenaline, charged forward like a force of nature.

With a primal yell, Sage lunged at Kamari as she tackled her to the ground. The gun clattered aside as they grappled, a desperate clash of wills. Sage's wound was forgotten in the chaos, as her instincts and rage overpowered the pain.

Meanwhile, Luke and Mylan guarded Warren. Their eyes darted between his wound and the chaos outside the casino. The sirens grew louder. Luke knew they had to act fast. "Shouldn't we stop this?" Luke glanced at Mylan.

Mylan's urgency was clear, driven by the need to avoid questions. "Listen, I've got to get out of here before the cops bust in here and start asking questions. Keep them under control." With a quick nod, he slipped out through the back exit, melting into the chaotic surroundings to avoid any unwanted attention.

Nora intervened, positioning herself between Sage and Kamari as they struggled for the gun. In a tense moment, all three of them lunged for the weapon. However, Kamari gained control. Her grip tightened around the firearm. Before they could react further, a gunshot rang out, and Nora staggered back. A pained cry escaped her lips as her leg was struck. Kamari's voice was laced with venom as she confronted Sage, gun raised. "I loved you."

A sudden commotion erupted as SWAT teams stormed into the casino. Following behind, Detectives Douglas and Matthew burst onto the scene. Amidst the chaos, Detective Douglas's voice boomed as he commanded, "Drop your weapon!"

Sage's and Kamari's eyes locked. A silent conversation passed between them. Sage's voice trembled with urgency as she implored, "Just put the gun down. They won't hesitate to shoot."

Nora rose above her own pain. Her wounded leg throbbed. With gritted teeth, she positioned herself between Kamari and the guns aimed their way, creating an unexpected barrier.

Kamari's confusion was obvious as she looked up at Nora. Her own internal battle mirrored the one she faced with the authorities. "What are you doing?" she asked

Nora's reply held a firmness that matched the unyielded intensity in her eyes. Her focus remained fixed on Kamari. "They have to get through me to get to you."

Her gaze shifted between Sage and Nora. "I'm not Sage," she insisted. Her eyes locked onto Nora's. "You can't trick me. I hate you," Kamari's words hung in the air, a raw expression of her wounded past.

Among them, Detectives Douglas and Matthew maneuvered with trained precision, their eyes locked onto Kamari and the unfolding drama.

"You mean nothing to me," Kamari's voice trembled. Her grip on the gun tightened, as she locked eyes with Nora, "I would rather be buried with my father than to live on this earth with a sister like you." the words were sharp.

Nora's voice wavered as she spoke, her eyes locked onto Kamari's. "I know I can't change the past, Kamari. I can't undo the pain I've caused you. But I'm standing here now, willing to make things right. You shot me, and I'm still here, wanting to protect you. I wanted none of this for either of us." Her voice held a plea.

Kamari's hand came down on her head. "No, no, no. Stop lying to me. You don't mean that."

Sage's voice carried a sincere and heartfelt tone. "If I can find it in myself to forgive, then I believe you can, too. We've both suffered because of her, but I'm ready to move forward. I only have one mother, and you only have one sister. Despite our flaws, we're still family. Please put the gun down."

Detective Douglas and Matthew, surrounded by a team of SWAT officers, had their guns trained on the three women. The tension in the air was almost tangible as the law enforcement officers maintained a cautious stance, ready to respond to any sudden movement. The flashing lights from the police vehicles outside painted the casino in alternating hues of red and blue.

Kamari brushed away her tears with a trembled hand. "I'm going to be locked up for a long time," she whispered, her voice quivered.

"I will be there," Nora murmured. She reached Kamari's hand and took the gun from her grip. As the weapon clattered to the floor, Nora enveloped her sister in a tight embrace. Tears streamed down Kamari's face as they held each other, emotions poured down like a stream of water.

Their connection was broken as the police intervened, as they pried Kamari away and led her off in handcuffs. Nora's heart ached as she watched her sister being taken away, yet a sense of relief surged through her. EMTs arrived to tend to their injuries, and they were all transported to the hospital for medical attention.

Chapter 29

Endings & Echoes

S age's steps reverberated through the hospital corridor, her anxiety tangible in the air. In the waiting room, Tegan, Cylus, Avery, and Luke sat together, the tension of the situation weaving a web of unease around them.

"Can you relax? You're making me nervous," Avery said with an eye roll, though her own apprehension couldn't be concealed.

Luke rose from his seat and placed a calming hand on Sage's shoulder. "Everything is going to be okay. Just breathe," he encouraged,

Cylus stepped closer to her, concern etched across his features. "Why are you so anxious? You know everything is going to be okay. She's a fighter."

Sage sighed, her worry clear in her eyes. "I know, but sometimes things can go wrong. Complications happen. And you know how these doctors can be, especially with black women.

They don't always prioritize our well-being; as long as the insurance goes through, right?"

Cylus gazed at her. Despite the heavy topic, Sage managed a faint smile, appreciating the support he offered in this uncertain moment.

Mylan's face lit up as he entered the waiting room, his grin infectious. "She's here," he announced, a sense of relief in his voice.

Nora arrived, her presence infused with a touch of urgency. "Sorry I'm late. I had to pick up a gift," she explained in a breathless tone. A quick peck was planted on Luke's lips before she joined Mylan, Avery, and Sage, leading the way to the hospital room.

They entered Sarah's room to find her cradling a beautiful baby girl in her arms. The room was filled with adoring glances and heartwarming smiles as they all took in the sight. "I'm officially an auntie," Nora quipped with a chuckle, placing the gifts she had brought on the nearby table.

Curiosity sparkled in her eyes, Avery leaned in closer. "What's her name?" she inquired, excited.

Sarah exchanged a meaningful glance with Mylan, their shared decision clear. "Laverne Charlotte Cooper," Sarah replied with a soft smile.

Avery's face lit up even more. "You named her after grandma," she noted, her joy obvious in her beaming smile.

Sage and Avery exchanged a joyful hug, their happiness radiating from their faces. Nora embraced Mylan with a sense of shared joy, their bond strengthened by the moment. Sarah and the newborn were surrounded by Avery and Sage's excitement, creating a warm and vibrant atmosphere for the whole family.

However, the joyful scene was interrupted by the ring on Nora's phone. She stepped out of the room to answer the call. "Hello," she greeted, her voice curious and attentive.

"Nora Woods. My name is Veronica Segan," a stern voice echoed through the phone. "Your daughter murdered my son, Que. Then your sister Kamari took money that she didn't deserve. You convinced Luke to kill his uncle and now he has full ownership of the casino. You have taken everything from me. I will stop at nothing until your entire family is destroyed." The line went silent as the call ended. Nora stared at her phone in shock, her heart pounded in her chest.

As Nora looked up, she noticed Luke approaching her with a concerned expression. A sense of terror engulfed her, and she felt a shiver down her spine, uncertain of what was to come.

The End.

"Do not take revenge, my dear friends, but leave room for God's wrath, for it is written: It is mine to avenge; I will repay," says the Lord."

Roman 12:19